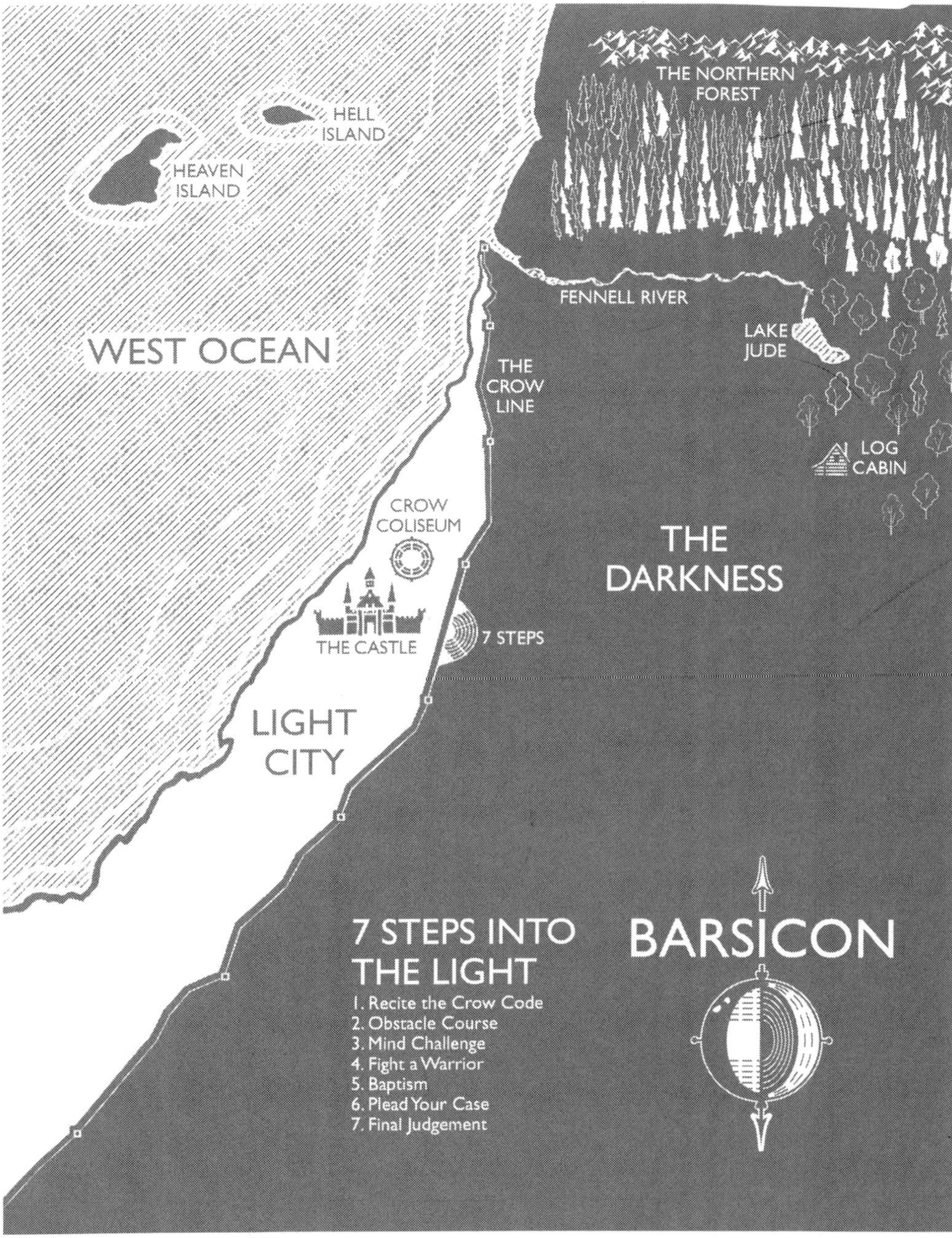
THE NORTHERN
FOREST
HELL
ISLAND
HEAVEN
ISLAND
FENNELL RIVER
LAKE
JUDE
WEST OCEAN
THE
CROW
LINE
LOG
CABIN
CROW
COLISEUM
THE
DARKNESS
THE CASTLE
7 STEPS
LIGHT
CITY
7 STEPS INTO
THE LIGHT
1. Recite the Crow Code
2. Obstacle Course
3. Mind Challenge
4. Fight a Warrior
5. Baptism
6. Plead Your Case
7. Final Judgement
BARSICON

CONQUERING THE DIVIDE

THE LEGEND OF BARSICON

ANGELA STEVER

Conquering the Divide

tellwell

Tellwell Talent
www.tellwell.ca

ISBN
978-0-2288-6313-7 (Hardcover)
978-0-2288-6312-0 (Paperback)
978-0-2288-6314-4 (eBook)

For my family.

All of you.

PROLOGUE

THE BATTLE OF BARSICON

Thursday, April 27th, 1972

Barsicon was crowded.

Quick pleasantries exchanged between upbeat folks hurrying off to dinner. A few market vendors allowed dawdling customers to complete last minute purchases before closing shop. Children played soccer anywhere there was space.

High above, Queen Raya stood on the balcony outside her luxurious bedroom in Jordhar Castle and admired the familiar scene. Fresh air filled her lungs as she drew in a purposeful breath, inhaling the season of hope.

Spring.

The sweet fragrance of new life.

Queen Raya overlooked the West Ocean from her grand perch and expressed gratitude to the universe for her incredible life. Barsicon was thriving. King Quinton was borderline perfect, as ruler, husband, and father to their two daughters.

Mildred and Matilda were identical twins. Both girls so remarkably wise for only having travelled around the sun seven times.

Mildred was calm, analytical and sweet.

Matilda was energetic, curious and often demanding. “She takes after you!” Quinton and Raya would say to one another.

The twins preferred to be called 'Millie' and 'Tilly' and she happily called them by their childhood monikers, aware the day would come when the girls would ask to be referred to by their full names. Maybe even take on different last names.

She freed her mind of such thoughts. Eventually, Mildred and Matilda would have to stand on their own two feet.

But not today.

As Queen Raya reflected on the balcony, a monarch butterfly fluttered down from the sky and landed on her nose. A pleasant kiss from Mother Nature.

"You always attract the animals." King Quinton grabbed his wife around the waist and pulled her in for his own pleasant kiss.

"Tell me about it." A devilish grin.

The King wrapped his arms around his wife. Their raven-coloured hair intertwined below the shoulders. Strands, interchangeable. Words, unnecessary.

The lovers and rulers of Barsicon admired their kingdom from high above.

Jordhar Castle had always been King Quinton's residence. However, the first day it felt like home was the day he married Raya. The day he made his queen, *the* Queen.

Her aqua eyes trapped him from the start. Queen Raya's authentic spirit beamed from her baby blue-greens. Their colour matched the West Ocean and the King was more than happy to drown in them.

Physically, Mildred and Matilda were miniature versions of their mother. Eye colour and all.

The exception was their pointy noses. An unreturnable gift from their father.

The King and Queen had been married for over a decade, and with each year that passed, their bond grew stronger.

Their attraction grew daily.

King Quinton brushed his fingertips along his wife's bare arms. Absolute softness. The only thing softer than her skin was her heart.

As Queen, she could live a lavish lifestyle in Jordhar Castle. Instead, she chose to go out and help the people who needed it most. Poverty was nonexistent in Barsicon. Raya would not allow it. There were no food shortages. No one lived on the streets. No stray animals searched for love or comfort. Everyone was cared for in her kingdom. Queen Raya made sure of that.

"Are you meeting with the council tonight?" she asked.

"No," he replied. "Walter just informed me of a delay. We'll be meeting tomorrow afternoon instead."

"Why the sudden change?"

"General Homer Thomson requested an emergency meeting with Walter. My hunch is he wants more money to expand his military again."

"You'll refuse like last time, right?" Queen Raya's forehead tensed with concern.

"Of course, darling. Barsicon has been a peaceful nation for centuries and our current military numbers are sufficient. Walter will put him straight tonight," he reassured her. "He knows where I stand."

Walter Crow was the King's right hand man and chair of the Royal Privy Council, a group of five men and women who governed Barsicon. Walter was a charming and ambitious 22-year-old, whose brilliant mind always appeared on fire because of his bright red hair.

King Quinton considered himself lucky to have that kind of genius close by. Not only did Walter have the answer to every seemingly impossible question, but he was also pure joy to have around the castle. That being said, he was the last person you wanted to play chess with.

Unless you enjoyed losing.

Queen Raya eyed her husband seductively. "Now that your presence is no longer required by the council, whatever shall we do to pass the time?"

King Quinton glanced over his shoulder into the bedroom. "I have a few ideas."

He carried his queen to their canopy bed, pulled back the sheer drapes and carefully placed her on top of red satin bedding. The first kiss he placed gently on her forehead. The next fell on her nose. He moved his lips to her mouth and neck, inching his way down her body before---*bang, bang!*

Fists pounded at the door. High-pitched screeches filled their ears. Mildred and Matilda broke through the wooden barrier and tumbled into the room.

"Mom! Dad! Can we stay up late and watch the dance in the town square from the balcony?"

"Pretty, pretty, pretty pleeeeeease?!"

"Not tonight, girls." Quinton's eyes pleaded with Raya for a raincheck. "Although there is something your mother and I would like to speak with you about."

"Your father and I have decided that tomorrow night we will not be watching the dance from the balcony."

Mildred was clearly confused. "But we always watch on Friday nights."

"This is SO UNFAIR!" screamed Matilda.

"Tilly, that's enough," he scolded. "Let your mother finish."

King Quinton raised an eyebrow in his wife's direction. They silently acknowledged the handful they had in Matilda.

"Millie and Tilly," she continued. "Tomorrow night, we will not be watching from the balcony because we are going down to the town square to dance with the community."

The girls gawked at their parents, silent for a fleeting moment.

Then came the squeals.

Raya immediately regretted telling them the news before bedtime. Getting the twins to settle in for the night was going to be difficult now.

As if reading her mind, King Quinton sent Mildred and Matilda on their way. "One hour until bedtime. Run along and finish your paintings."

Queen Raya ushered the girls out the door. "Nightgowns and storytime after that. Let's go."

Within moments of the door closing behind the twins, the lovers were back in each other's arms. It would take more than a small interruption to erase the longing they had for one another.

Her hands cupped his face. She traced her fingers through his thick, black beard. Thinking of that thing she did with her chin that drove him wild, Quinton released Raya for a split second to lock the door and avoid any future intrusions. He didn't loosen his grip on her again until they were both blissfully satisfied.

At last, the King was forced to let go, fully aware that ignoring the telephone on the nightstand wouldn't get it to stop ringing. Whoever it was, they were persistent.

"Hello?"

It was Walter. "King Quinton, your presence is requested by General Homer Thompson. Once again, he's demanding an increase in frontline soldiers. I've expressed our position but he insists on hearing it straight from you."

"The message comes from me. What part of that does he not understand? Tell Homer if he wants to meet with me personally, he can set up a meeting."

"One second."

Whispers in the background.

"Does eight o'clock work?"

It certainly wasn't ideal. King Quinton hated morning meetings. But he couldn't avoid the General forever, especially now that he was demanding a face-to-face. Besides, it was unfair of him to make Walter deal with this alone.

"Eight o'clock it is." The King slammed the phone down on the receiver.

"Is everything okay?"

"The General won't take no for an answer from Walter. He's demanding to meet with me tomorrow morning."

"Who is he to make demands? I don't like the way Homer's been acting these past few months, Quinton. He's been extremely bold and aggressive. To put it mildly."

"You've noticed too, huh?"

She slipped a smooth leg between his thighs. "Perhaps it's time he was put in his place by my King."

"Perhaps."

Queen Raya rested her head on his heart and allowed the steady beat to lull her close to sleep.

King Quinton ended their post-coital snuggle. "It won't be long now before the twins come demanding their bedtime stories."

He was right, but she wasn't ready to let go.

For a few more breaths, she basked in the euphoria that consumed her entire being when she was with him. If these were her final breaths, she would die a happy woman.

Brimming with love, Raya squeezed her husband tight one last time.

Bedtime stories were told separately to appease the twins. The girls were identical in appearance but polar opposites in their interests. Matilda wanted to be entertained with epic sagas of dragons and war. Mildred favoured unicorns and fairytale endings.

However, they both loved to hear stories about the mysterious giants from the Northern Forest.

King Quinton tucked Matilda into bed, while Queen Raya took Mildred onto the balcony and allowed her a glimpse of the street party below.

"Millie, don't tell your sister."

"I promise," she giggled. "I won't tell Tilly."

Only one of her princesses would rub that in.

It was not Mildred.

"Okay, it's almost eight o'clock. Climb into my bed. I'll tell you the story about the magical dogs and the gentle giants from beyond the trees."

Mildred snuggled in next to her mother.

"Once upon a time, on a bright and sunny afternoon, Princess Millie went for a walk in the Northern Forest."

Down the hall, King Quinton told Matilda a similar tale, trading out magical dogs for ferocious wolves and not-so-gentle giants.

"It was a dark and stormy night when Tilly snuck away from Jordhar Castle and entered the thick brush in the Northern Forest," he started.

Less than fifty feet away, the Queen continued her tale. "As Millie walked along the clear path, she heard the pitter-patter of paws and saw the cutest Roxy dogs running towards her. Fortunately, she had brought along some treats for her new friends."

Back in the twins' bedroom, the King's voice grew louder. "Tilly tore her way through thick brush. Her heart pounded. The sounds of Ferox Caninovours moved closer. They could smell the extra cookie in Tilly's pocket. The one she had taken from the dessert tray after dinner."

Matilda shrunk. She didn't think her father had noticed her swipe a third gingersnap. King Quinton didn't address it any further. For now, it was enough that she knew he knew.

"Tilly threw the cookie far into the forest and watched the hungry Ferox Caninovours tear each other apart trying to devour it. During the commotion, she climbed the nearest tree, where she hid until the wolves left and all was quiet again. But all was not quiet for long. Heavy footsteps crept closer."

"Just then, a giant as tall as the trees came into view. He picked her up in his hand so they were eye to eye. Then the giant asked

Millie if she wanted to join him and his family for a treehouse dinner!"

Queen Raya looked at the clock on the nightstand. The little hand pointed at the number eight and the big hand shot directly north. Time to wrap this story up before Mildred fell asleep in their bed again. Already, her daughter's eyelids were spending more time together than apart.

Startled by a knock at the door, Queen Raya rose from bed to see a man in uniform enter the room. She quickly drew heavy black drapes around one side of the bed to shield herself, and more importantly, to protect Mildred from the sudden intruder.

"Get under the covers and stay there." She tossed pillows on top of blankets to hide her daughter's small silhouette. "Do not come out until I tell you it's safe."

The two soldiers in charge of guarding the hallway followed the military man inside and closed the door behind them.

Why hadn't they stopped him from entering?

Queen Raya closed her robe and attempted to hide the fear rising within her. "Excuse me, General Thomson. What gives you the right to barge in here at this hour? Or any hour for that matter."

"I have a meeting with your husband at eight o'clock." Homer looked down at his wrist. "According to my watch, he's one minute late."

"King Quinton scheduled you for a morning meeting. Even still, that gives you no right to invade my privacy."

"Oh, I believe it does," he snarled. "Guess we'll just have to agree to disagree on this one."

"Remember who you are speaking to. Have some respect, Homer. I am the Queen of Barsicon. What world do you live in where it's acceptable behaviour to enter a queen's bedchamber unannounced and undermine her authority?"

General Thomson started towards her.

Instincts told her to back away.

Instead, Raya took three steps in his direction to create distance between the soldiers and Mildred.

"I said, what world do you live in..."

The military leader cleared the space between them, grabbed her by the throat and slammed her against the wall.

"I live in *my* world, you mouthy bitch!" General Thomson spat in her face.

Their noses practically touched. Queen Raya could taste his sweat. Calloused hands wrapped tight around her neck. With every bit of strength she could muster, she called out to King Quinton. Her cries only made the General squeeze tighter.

She grimaced in pain.

Had Homer already killed Quinton and Matilda? After he murdered her, he might find Mildred hiding in the bed. By the strength of his grip and the hatred in his eyes, one thing was certain.

General Thomson would not let go until she was dead.

The faces of her family were the last Queen Raya wanted to envision when her soul left her body. She replaced her killer's face with cherished memories of her husband and daughters. Flashes of family dinners and playtime at the beach. Close-ups of their faces, forever etched into her spirit.

Unfortunately, they were not the last image she would see before darkness took hold.

A man rushed into the room as she drew her final breath.

In the end, it was Walter Crow's stunned face imprinted in her mind when the undulating aqua waves in Queen Raya's ocean eyes came to a final halt.

PART I

CHAPTER 1

FAREWELL, DAVID

Saturday, October 22nd, 2005

President Barbara Crow could spot a troublemaker from a mile away. These two were both troublemakers. She eyed the television monitor closely. Watched, as the couple said goodbye.

"If only you knew this was your final farewell," she scoffed to an empty study.

There were cameras on every corner in Light City. President Barbara Crow could tap into them anytime she pleased. Her favourite feed to watch was from the Waiting Room, where Light Seekers said goodbye to their families before the weekly Light Ceremony.

Most of the final meetings were upbeat and positive. The Waiting Room filled with folks who were thrilled at the prospect of living in Light City before the end of the night.

However, others were gripped by fear and anxiety. Loved ones crying on the same shoulders they had placed the weight of the world on.

Their futures depended on their Light Seeker completing all Seven Steps into the Light.

It was their only hope to escape The Darkness.

Occasionally, a Light Seeker and their family could tell they were being watched. Today's pair seemed completely oblivious to the president's prying, electronic eyes.

For some reason, it gave Barbara intense joy to observe desperate peasants in such heartfelt moments. Convinced they had a say in their own futures.

The Waiting Room was inside the Crow Line; a massive wall that separated Light City from The Darkness. Her father, General Walter Crow, had demanded the wall's construction following the Battle of Barsicon in 1972. It took the Northern Warriors months to erect the barrier, which ran parallel to the coastline, a mere two miles inland from the West Ocean.

The wall reached high into the sky, blocking off ocean access to everyone living east of it.

No worries, the people said. They still had clean lakes and rivers on their side of the divide.

Eventually, the wall grew tall enough to block out the sun hours before sunset, which is how the land on the east side came to be known as The 'Darkness'.

Despite losing several hours of direct sunlight in the morning, no one in Light City noticed the change.

If they did, they didn't mention it.

Only the well-to-do lived along the West Ocean. The city was populated with residents who would sleep until noon and feast until midnight. Folks who would play games and dance all day. Most of whom would barely stop to admire a breath-taking sunset from their balcony high above the cliffs lining the coastline.

These people didn't complain about the wall. They loved it. The Crow Line gave them a sense of security.

Protection from the 'unworthy'.

The Crow Line wasn't just home to the Waiting Room. It also housed the Northern Warriors when they were on duty. These massive men lived in windowless rooms with high ceilings and few amenities. Two weeks on patrol in Light City. Then two weeks back home in the Northern Forest.

Inside the Waiting Room, there were two doors. One swung into The Darkness and the other led into Light City. In the centre of the room was a large wooden table with eight matching chairs. They had been hand-carved by the city's master carpenter, Heather Jean. Her works were coveted throughout Light City and President Crow had her on speed dial. No matter the need or the want, the best in Barsicon was at her beck and call 24/7.

Barbara eavesdropped on the lovebirds in the Waiting Room, listening as the Light Seeker spewed promises to the beautiful blonde woman. Promises he couldn't possibly keep. Ultimately, his fate was in Barbara's hands and she had decided *not* to let him keep his word.

Or his life.

"Stop shaking, my love!"

Shaking? Her entire body was trembling.

"Kate, are you okay? You look so scared."

Not scared. Terrified, Barbara thought. Terrified of not getting into Light City. Horrified at the thought of having to go back to The Darkness.

Who could blame her?

"Come on, Kate. Give me a little smile at least?"

The woman tried on a halfhearted grin.

It didn't fit.

"Today is an exciting day! It's the day I secure our future in Light City. I'm going to have you back home by the end of the day. Promise."

A small jump and he was on top of the table. A goofy smile smeared across his chiseled face.

Go easy on that table, Barbara silently scolded.

"I'm sorry, David. I'm just feeling a bit anxious. I have so much faith in you!"

"I love you," David professed to his wife, placing both hands on her stomach.

"I love you too. I can't wait to see you on the other side of this wall. To start our new life together." She placed her hands on top of his. "All of us."

"Kate, I promise you this isn't the end. It's just the beginning."

"No, it's the end," said Barbara. "Obadiah!"

Her brother stumbled into the study. No matter where the oaf was in their massive castle, he could hear her voice.

Obadiah removed his hat, lowered his eyes and peered down at their silk Isfahan rug. Barely in his twenties, the bald spot on the crown of his head expanded with each sunrise.

At least the oaf had been blessed with their mother's dark hair. Barbara would kill for Tilly's long, black locks. Instead, she'd been cursed with Walter's twisted flames.

"Hi, Barbara."

"Obadiah, come sit. Take a moment with me, would you?"

Barbara took her brother's hat from his hands, placed it back on his head with a few friendly shakes of the brim and ushered him over to the settee.

"Sit down and I'll grab you some water. It looks like you've been working hard today."

"Yes, ma'am," Obadiah grinned from ear to ear.

She didn't deserve his love. He wouldn't even be this way if it wasn't for her.

Barbara poured her brother a tall glass of ice water and handed it to him. Obadiah guzzled it. Streams of water spilled from his mouth.

Outside the corner picture window was a jaw-dropping view of the West Ocean. Barsicon had been Barbara's baby for three years now. When she was 22 years old, she took over the presidency from her father, who still used dinnertime at Crow Castle to ramble on about what priorities she should focus on.

But for the most part, it seemed Walter respected and trusted her. Maybe someday he would also *love* her again.

Her brother finished his water and sat quietly, awaiting his next order.

"All done?"

"Yes, ma'am." Obadiah handed her the empty glass.

The Light Ceremony was about to get underway. Barbara still hadn't made the call. Of course, she had come to a decision in her mind. She simply hadn't relayed it to anyone.

"Obadiah. I need you to tell the cloud operator that we don't need him today. We'll be ending the ceremony on the fifth step. Is that understood?"

"Fifth step. Tell cloud operator no work. End on fifth step."

"Yes. Also, we're going to keep this one today. If we can."

"End on fifth step. Keep this one."

"Very good. You're dismissed."

Obadiah jumped up and headed toward the front door of their cliffside castle, eager to complete his next task.

The Light Ceremony was minutes away now and her presence was required. Perfect. She couldn't think of a better way to spend a Saturday evening.

President Barbara Crow tossed her white ceremonial cloak overtop of her black dress and left the study.

It was time to say goodbye to this week's Light Seeker.

Two giants dragged David's limp body from the baptism tank.

The love of her life, now lifeless.

How did this happen?

David promised he would come back to her. They were supposed to live together in Light City.

Happily ever after.

The only thing she could think to do was run. She couldn't face David's sister or his friends. They had always supported David's life decisions, but she knew they weren't thrilled with him becoming a Light Seeker.

Now that he was gone, the blame would fall squarely on her and she couldn't deal with it.

So, she ran.

Kate!!!

She heard them calling her name. It didn't slow her. Her mind shut off and her legs took over. One foot in front of the other, building speed until she was in a full-on sprint. Was shock the reason no tears would fall? David was gone and the only thing she could do was run.

"Hey, lady. Watch it!"

She stumbled forward, her balance thrown off kilter when she slammed into a stranger. Dust kicked up in her face.

Back on your feet. Run!

Full of adrenaline, she kept pace at a sprint. Out of breath, lungs on fire, she moved forward. Thankfully, she couldn't feel her legs anymore. The elegant walking sticks she normally controlled now had a mind of their own. And a clear destination.

There was one person in The Darkness who wasn't close to David. The only person she could turn to for guidance. For help. She would need all the help she could get.

Closer and closer. Almost there.

Please be home.

The stone cottage was within sight.

A light was on!

Her legs gave out from under her the second she reached the doorstep. She was too exhausted to knock. Not that she needed to. The woman would know she was there.

As expected, the door opened seconds later. "Kate, my dear girl. Take my hand. Let's get you inside."

Limitless white hair sprouted from the elderly woman's head, slid down her back and touched her ankles. Her solid purple dress lacked shape, so she created some by adding a belt.

If you could call a piece of rope a belt.

"I'm just finishing up with someone in the kitchen. Warm yourself by the fire and I'll be right with you."

She was happy to sit. This had been the longest day of her life and she was weary. Weak. By the time her wrinkled friend returned minutes later, she was fast asleep.

CHAPTER 2

A LIGHT SEEKER NAMED SENECA

Wednesday, July 6th, 2022

Seneca Ellis-Brant waited until her back was turned to both of her mothers before she rolled her eyes. They rolled so far back, she was convinced the two women had spotted her hazel sightseers from across the kitchen.

"I won't be long," she promised.

She took extra care not to slam the screen door. No need to upset her royal highness, Catherine Ellis. Or as Seneca commonly referred to her, 'Mama C'.

The young Light Seeker lifted her bicycle from the exact spot on the lawn she had pitched it the night before. She pushed the long side of her coffee-coloured hair behind her ear, stuck her hand inside the bottom half of her stained white t-shirt and used it to dry the seat.

Riding in wet jeans was a recipe for a rash.

Light Seeker training was over for the day and she needed to escape, get away from her mothers and all their 'Seven Steps' talk.

"I would take your place in a heartbeat if I could!"

That would be Mama C.

"I'm almost jealous that *you* get to be the one. Is that bad to say?"

Yes, Catherine. That's terrible to say.

Thankfully, Ma Marie always took a gentler approach.

"To be a Light Seeker is a great honour, Seneca. Few mortals possess the physical, mental, emotional and spiritual wherewithal to even attempt all Seven Steps into the Light. The Creator has bestowed upon you the gifts needed for reparation. To make such a sacrifice for one's family is the ultimate life achievement."

Easier said than done.

Mama C and Ma Marie weren't the ones who had to survive all Seven Steps on their own. She needed to breathe. Escape for a few hours and clear her mind.

Marie yelled after her as she pedaled away from their log cabin. "Be back by 6 o'clock, Sen. Ribs tonight. Your favourite."

Ribs? They couldn't afford ribs. She must have traded something good for those.

"And don't be late or we'll eat them without you!"

Marie's attempt to sound playful failed. Seneca rode away without turning back. She didn't need to see Ma's face to know the stress she was under. It was evident in her voice. Despite Ma's best effort to hide it, she could still hear that telltale quiver.

All the more reason to get out of here for the afternoon. Soon she would be down by the river, skipping stones, climbing trees, and avoiding the harsh reality that three days from now she could be dead.

Yes, ribs would be good tonight.

A steep hill led to her favourite spot by the river. Seneca reached the top and stopped pedaling. Gravity could handle the job from here. Steadying herself, she closed both eyes and let go of the handlebars, stretching her arms from east to west. She remained that way, as free as a blind bird, until her front tire touched the grassy knoll feet from the river.

Seneca launched off nature's ramp and ditched her two-wheeler in mid-air. She opened her eyes in time to see her bike fall to the shoreline. Her body plunged into the water feet first and created an unusually big splash.

By the time she resurfaced amid the waves, her mind was clear.

The afternoon sun beat down on her face. Seneca submitted to the water. She let go of all her worries and allowed the current to pull her along at its will.

As she drifted in the direction of Light City, she felt carefree. She wasn't worried about the sun beating down on her skin. Or what Catherine would have to say about direct sun exposure.

"Cover up. Otherwise, you'll end up with Ma Marie's skin."

That was a confusing statement. For one, she already had Marie's light brown skin tone. Not to mention Ma absolutely glowed. Most people would kill for her smooth, bronze skin. Catherine was downright pasty.

Pasty... and jealous?

It was easy to tell Catherine was originally from Light City. She had royalty written all over her. The difficult part was imagining Catherine moving to The Darkness because she was so in love with Marie.

Much of Seneca's childhood had been spent listening to Catherine ramble on about how magnificent it would be living back home again. The smell of the ocean. The cutting-edge technology. Not to mention the feasts, the fabrics and the fabulous people.

So, so many mentions.

Now, they were close.

In three days, she would stand in front of thousands of people and earn their way into Light City.

Or die.

Dying wasn't the optimal outcome, obviously. But at least she wouldn't be around to witness her moms' disappointment if she did fail. They could be trying at times, especially Catherine, but she loved them so much. They believed with their whole hearts that she was their miracle child.

Born to seek the light.

The thought of letting them down made her sick to her stomach.

It was her growling tummy that brought her back to the present. Ribs were being served soon and the sun was going down over the Crow Line.

It was time to head home.

Seneca trudged through the river in water-logged jeans and found her bike floating along the shoreline. No drying off the seat this time. She hopped on, pedaled up the hill and prayed Ma Marie would have some ointment to soothe her impending rash.

CHAPTER 3

THE PRESIDENT'S PLAN

Seneca opened the door as carefully as she had closed it on her way out. President Barbara Crow's voice blasted out of the old black and white television in the kitchen. Her moms were glued to the six o'clock news.

"It pains me to see an increase in the crime rate in Light City. For many years, we proudly boasted a zero percent crime rate. Yet in the last month, police have investigated three crimes. Three! An innocent young man was assaulted..."

That voice. Talk about nails on a chalkboard.

"...and therefore, next week I will unveil my new plan for crime and punishment. It has become apparent that banishing criminals to The Darkness is no longer a strong enough deterrent. Change is coming to keep all of us safe. No further comments until the official news conference. Thank you and God bless those who walk in the light."

The election was quickly approaching and the President's nightly news updates were sounding more like pre-election speeches.

Which was totally unnecessary considering she was running unopposed.

Throughout her 20-year reign, not a single candidate stepped forward to run against Barbara. Only one person attempted it in the thirty years prior, when Barbara's father Walter had been in charge.

In half a century, only *one* man was brave enough to throw his hat in the ring.

That man would never wear a hat again, what with his head being split in two and all.

Some say the axe was still resting between his surprised eyes when they found his body hanging off the seventh step at the Light City gates. Rumour was, his surprised look had little to do with the fact that he was about to be murdered and more to do with *who* was about to execute him.

Stories shared in the streets told of an angry teenaged Barbara holding the axe.

Again, just rumours.

Not a single soul in Light City expressed political aspirations after that. It was smooth sailing for the Crow family. An election was still held every five years, but it was more of a formality. A ceremony of sorts.

The Crows were big on their ceremonies.

Seneca had watched the election on television twice. She was eleven the last time. Marie had made a special blueberry pie and Catherine allowed her to take a few sips of wine.

For whatever reason, she laughed a lot that day!

The election was a spectacle to watch, even on television. Every resident in Light City gathered to witness it at Crow Coliseum.

The massive outdoor stadium seated 80,000. It was built as a gathering place for the people of Light City, but it was more than that.

Crow Coliseum stood as a symbol of the Crow family's power.

The election was an extravagant affair. A highlight every half decade for those who respected the Crow family, and many did. Anticipation grew in the days leading up to the event. Reporters camped outside of the coliseum and interviewed anyone who agreed to be a talking head.

Even as a child, Seneca thought their questions were ridiculous.

"What do you think President Crow will be wearing? Will she be late again like she was in 2017? Bookies have three-to-one odds

Walter and Matilda will be wearing matching outfits like in 2012. Good enough for you to put some money down?"

Seneca wished she was the reporter asking the questions. She wanted to know why no one ran against the Crow family. Why they thrived on separation between Light City and The Darkness.

Most importantly, she wanted to know why there were still people in The Darkness working day in and day out just to survive, while playing neighbour to extreme excess in the west. It made no sense to her.

Why were some people 'born into the light', while others had to risk their lives for the same opportunity?

If Seneca lived to see the next election, perhaps she would ask President Crow herself.

Lately, she'd been having recurring daydreams about challenging the president during the election ceremony. When her mind wandered, her imagination took her to Crow Coliseum to the moment when President Crow made her royal entrance onto the platform.

In real life, the president addressed the crowd at the climax of the ceremony and asked the same question each time.

"Is there a soul among us who wishes to challenge my leadership?"

No one in the crowd dared to breathe. Not even those watching on television from deep in The Darkness. Seneca remembered sitting on the living room floor as a child, holding her breath for the mandatory ten seconds of silence observed before the president concluded the ceremony with the standard Crow family motto.

"God bless those who walk in the light."

In her daydream, Barbara never made it to that part because Seneca spoke up.

"I challenge you."

"Challenge me to what? Are you listening..."

"Uhhhh."

Catherine had ordered her to do something. Now she had to figure out what that something was.

She flashed her dimples innocently at her mother, who was growing more impatient by the second with her inaction.

"Stop giving me that look and get on with it! The table isn't going to set itself."

There it was.

A bit of patience and the answers will come to you.

Seneca searched the cupboard for three plates with no chips or cracks. She found two. The unmarked plates she placed in front of Catherine and Marie's spots at the table. The cracked one she kept for herself.

The line down the middle of her plate reminded her of the wall that separated Barsicon. As she stared at it, a map began to form. She envisioned Light City and the West Ocean on one side. Their log cabin in The Darkness on the other. Two worlds, separated by the Crow Line.

The crack made the plate weak.

Fragile.

Gasp!

The plate shattered in her hands. How tightly had she been gripping it? There must be hundreds of pieces on the floor.

"Oh, dear! Are you hurt?" Catherine panicked.

"I'm fine. Can't say the same for the plate."

"Don't move until I grab a broom."

Standing alone in the kitchen with shards of ceramic surrounding her feet, Seneca prayed her world wouldn't be the next thing to come crashing down around her.

CHAPTER 4

DINNER IN THE DARKNESS

After dinner, her taste buds still tingling with delight, Seneca challenged her mothers to a round of '99'. It was a popular card game in The Darkness. Many people had lost copious amounts of cash playing it.

They never placed bets on games around the kitchen table, but the winner had the pleasure of showering, while the other two cleaned up from dinner. That night, it was Catherine who rinsed away the day's filth, while Seneca and Marie tidied up.

Marie tossed her dish towel to the side and sat down to finish the daily crossword puzzle. "We'll let God dry 'em tonight."

That was her classic line and it always made Seneca giggle.

"Dinner was delicious. Thanks, Ma. Nothing like ribs falling off the bone. Mouthwatering stuff."

"My pleasure," Marie said, holding back tears from drenching paper clues on the table in front of her. "For the next three days, stay focused on everything we have taught you. There is no doubt in my mind you will complete each step with grace and redeem our family."

Seneca smiled. Tranquil on the outside. Troubled within.

"I'll give it my all."

"My daughter. The youngest Light Seeker in the history of Barsicon. I'm already so proud of..." Marie trailed off, choking on unspoken words.

She couldn't look at her mother. Instead, she continued scrubbing the same clean plate. A looser grip this time around.

Time to change the subject.

"Will they have a house for us when we get to Light City or will we stay somewhere temporarily? It seems like all of the houses are oceanside. What do you think our first meal will be?"

"We'll find out soon enough."

"Cheer up, Ma. You know I've got this. It's my destiny, right?"

"Yes," Marie brightened. "Three days from now, we'll walk through the gates of Light City together, hand in hand. An unstoppable trio! Are you ready?"

Seneca refused to allow her face to reflect the panic growing within. "More ready than I'll ever be."

"Good," said Marie. "We'll go over the steps again first thing tomorrow morning. If all goes well, we can break after lunch and take the boat out for the afternoon."

Sailing the Fennell River was one of Seneca's favourite things to do. As a child, she had watched Marie construct the family sailboat by hand. It was a machine and a work of art. Marie had named the boat 'Fee Fee', which seemed to have significance that clearly annoyed Catherine.

Then again, Mama C was annoyed by most things.

Their log cabin was closer to Lake Jude, but Marie insisted they dock Fee Fee on the Fennell River, an extra two miles down the road.

"The winds are stronger on the river," Ma would say confidently.

The Fennell River connected to the West Ocean. Not that Marie ever took the boat out there. As a resident of The Darkness, she wasn't allowed. What she could do was sail past the estuary and it was a decent view of the ocean from that vantage point.

Each time they sailed close to the mouth, Seneca would plead with her mom to slow down. She wanted to soak in the ocean's energy. Fantasize about the day Fee Fee would sail on the other side of the estuary.

Free.

For this to happen, she would have to manage her way through all Seven Steps into the Light and fulfill her destiny.

No big deal, right?

Seneca suddenly felt heavy. Like she was carrying the weight of the world on her shoulders and then some.

She kissed Marie goodnight and headed to bed.

Before sleep, a short prayer. "Dear God of Light. Grant me the strength to endure the next few days. I do enjoy talking to you every night, but I don't care to meet you anytime soon. Amen."

CHAPTER 5
HELLO, JD

Thursday, July 7th, 2022

The aroma of oats cooking on the stove brought Seneca to life the next morning. It was her final training day as a Light Seeker. The significance didn't elude her. Before her feet touched the floor, she took a moment to mentally prepare for the day ahead.

"Be strong," she told herself, drawing in a deep breath and holding it in for a minute before slowly releasing the air from her lungs. "This is your destiny."

It was so surreal. In a matter of hours, she would conclude a lifetime of training. Rehearse the Seven Steps one last time. Well, the first six anyway. No one was ignorant to the fact that it was truly impossible to prepare for the seventh step.

The God of Light's Final Judgement.

From the sky's hue, she guessed it was six o'clock in the morning. The Crow Line couldn't obstruct her view of the sunrise. She knew it was Marie cooking at this hour. There was no way Catherine would get out of bed before breakfast was served. Her passion for beauty sleep ran deep.

Seneca slid her feet into a pair of handknit slippers and trudged sleepy-eyed into the kitchen, hugging Marie from behind as she hovered over the hot stove.

"Good morning, sweetie. Breakfast is almost ready."

Resting her head on Marie's back, Seneca felt the kind of warmth only a loved one gives off, and she took a moment to bask in the warm glow. Then she headed straight to the refrigerator. If there was one thing she could always rely on, it was a glass of freshly squeezed orange juice waiting for her each morning.

All of Barsicon's fresh crops were grown in The Darkness. Oranges were plentiful. Strawberries, grapes, and walnuts all thrived, as well as figs, apricots and pistachios.

Unfortunately, that didn't mean everyone had access to fresh fare.

Food was controlled by the Crow family. Most of what was grown in The Darkness was trucked to Light City. Some of it stayed to be sold at the market, but prices were high and paychecks were low.

Thankfully, anyone could grow food on their own property. Marie had planted several crops to help sustain them, limiting trips to the market, and ensuring Seneca woke to a thirst-quenching glass of OJ from their orange grove.

She sat at the table and watched Marie float around the kitchen, every movement effortless. Maybe someday she would be as confident and capable as Ma was.

Being raised as a Light Seeker was no easy task. Seneca had her moms and her combat instructor JD to thank for preparing her so well. The youngest Light Seeker before her was eighteen years old. His name was Jax and he didn't make it past the fourth step. Killed by a warrior's sword. That was before JD took over combat training for all Light Seekers. Thankfully, Seneca was trained by him and he was the best.

Even better for her, the best lived right next door.

Jamie Daniels was his full name. Everyone called him JD, at his request. There was a strange superstition in The Darkness that you shouldn't trust a man with two first names. Oddly enough, apart from her moms, Jamie Daniels was the only person Seneca trusted with her life. Or at least trusted enough to train her to save her own life.

Either way, they were both focused on keeping her alive.

The first time she spotted JD, Marie had to tell her that it was rude to stare at a person so long. Seneca couldn't look away. They were practically eye to eye.

JD stood about five feet, two inches.

On a tall day.

When they met, his neon-coloured mohawk was yellow and green. Today's colours were anyone's guess. He switched it up frequently, always going for extra style points.

Later this morning, she would spar with JD.

But first, breakfast.

"Anything I can do to help?" she offered.

"I believe mama bear is still fast asleep in her royal den. What do you say? Should one of us attempt to rouse her grizzly highness?"

"I guess I will," Seneca muttered, sounding as though she had lost a terrible bet.

The truth was, she was happy to do it. It would be one of the last times she would wake Mama C in their log cabin. Perhaps one of the last times she woke her, period.

That idea made her stomach flip.

Praying a hearty breakfast would pacify it, Seneca stood up from the table and set off to wake the bear.

CHAPTER 6

FATE VS DESTINY

The front porch creaked. Seneca swayed back and forth in a rickety rocking chair while she waited for Catherine, who would have ditched the old rocker long ago if Marie hadn't insisted they keep it around.

"A simple broken rail. No big fuss. I'll fix it up."

It would take several hours to rehearse the steps. Despite some nerves that were becoming increasingly hard to control, Seneca was prepared. Each night she prayed to the God of Light and begged for mercy on the fifth step.

The Baptism.

A person could only hold their breath for so long! Four minutes was her sweet spot. Then she started to struggle. If she factored in adrenaline, she was convinced she could survive six, maybe seven minutes.

Her fear of the fifth step stemmed from witnessing baptisms that lasted anywhere from twelve seconds to twelve minutes!

It was unpredictable.

Only the seventh step held more uncertainty and there was no shame following the last step. You were either a successful Light Seeker or dead.

Light Seekers whose baptisms lasted more than three minutes were looked down on by the mob of Barsiconians who watched the weekly event. A mix of folks from Light City and The Darkness. The fifth step was a cleansing of the soul and if your soul took longer than the average three minutes to clean, it was obviously filthy.

Watching the Light Ceremonies on Saturday nights was one of the best ways to study. That being said, she couldn't watch the baptisms without her heart pounding. A sense of relief always washed over her when a Light Seeker successfully completed their soul cleansing.

One step closer to fulfilling their destiny.

The meaning of destiny was taught to her by JD when she was 11 years old. She was having trouble mastering a new grappling technique and started to cry for the first time in years.

"Let's take five. Sit by the pond with me. When you're ready, tell me what bothers you," JD had said calmly.

Seneca didn't know how to respond. She didn't even know *why* she was crying. Was learning new grappling techniques really that frustrating? No, she would master them soon enough.

So what was it?

Before long she was spitting out words between sobs. Using JD's ears as a dumping ground for all her worries and doubts. Fears, hidden for years, resurfaced.

"What if I can't hold my breath long enough during practice today? Catherine was so disappointed yesterday when I didn't hit three minutes. I'm just getting over a cold. What if..."

"Seneca, slow down. You're worrying again! Like I always say, worrying is like praying for something bad to happen. Less negative energy toward the problem. Focus on positive solutions!" said JD, as though it were really that easy.

His enthusiasm annoyed her at times.

"What if I can't do this?"

"The grappling? You're doing great!"

"No, not that."

"Are you worried about your baptism? Please child. You still have years to train. Does Catherine use breathing techniques with you? If not, we can go over that at lunch today."

They always ate lunch together after their morning sessions. JD raised chickens next door, giving him an open invite to their kitchen table.

"No, I mean what if I can't get my family into Light City. What if my fate is death? I certainly wouldn't be the first."

The odds were pretty much 50/50. Not in Seneca's particular case. Those were the odds for all who went before her in search of the light.

"What if your fate is death? We all die, dear. Death is all our fates. Don't worry about fate, okay? Instead, let me help you understand *destiny*."

That day, JD taught Seneca that to live by fate was to go through life believing you are being controlled by circumstances beyond your control. Frustrating indeed! To follow your destiny was something different. Something special. It was about honouring your spiritual heritage. Accepting with your mind, body, heart and soul, that you came into this world with a clear purpose.

From that day forward, while Seneca studied and trained, she thought a lot about destiny and decided she would fully commit to hers.

Viewing it any other way made daily life overwhelming.

It was easier to train with the mindset, 'I'm doing this to fulfill my destiny', rather than doing it so she didn't 'go way of all flesh'. An expression she had overheard some of the elders use.

Seneca was undaunted by the first step. She had memorized the entire Crow Code forward and backward, inside and out, before her eighth birthday.

The Crow Code was made up of the Ten Crow Convictions. They were the most important rules in Light City.

Those who lived in The Darkness were able to choose their faith, but for those who lived along the West Ocean, religion wasn't a choice. Light City residents were practicing Crowians. Otherwise, they were banished to the other side of the Crow Line.

Crowianity was a newer religion. General Walter Crow introduced it fifty years ago, after experiencing a spiritual epiphany. According to the history books, Walter was visited by the God of Light himself in 1972.

That's when the new rules were written.

In addition to the Crow Convictions, there were also thousands of so-called 'basic principles'. To Seneca, there was nothing basic about them. She found them confusing and contradictory. In any case, she knew them by heart and was confident when tested.

That was Catherine's job.

Mama C helped her master the odd-numbered steps. JD handled combat training. Marie prepped her on the second and sixth steps. They always started from step one and worked their way up.

Marie insisted Seneca think of the steps in order.

The toughest transition was moving from fighting on the fourth step to holding her breath on the fifth.

Just two more times. Once in training today. Once more on Saturday night.

The real deal.

Catherine appeared in the doorway. "Ready?"

"All set."

She rocked herself out of the chair and gave her mom a quick kiss on the cheek. They set off to the gardens to sit amidst the flowers and go over the Crow Code one last time.

CHAPTER 7

FINAL TRAINING DAY

While children in Light City read stories about princes and princesses, puppies and ponies, Seneca studied the Crow Code. It was the last thing she did before bed each night and the first she tackled each morning.

Training was six days a week. Sunday was a rest day for her, as the God of Light commanded of everyone.

On a typical training day, start time was six o'clock. Up at five-thirty, breakfast, stretch and off to the garden. Most days, Catherine would stumble into the kitchen at 5:59 a.m. and grab a coffee to go.

"We do this for fifteen minutes a day and then you guys play around on that jungle gym for an hour," she'd complain. "Can't we do it at the end of the day?"

"The steps must be practiced in order," Marie would remind her. "We made that decision years ago."

"I don't understand why you can't instruct her on the first step and I'll take over the pleading of her case."

"Changing the routine helps no one. Surely you can sacrifice a little bit of beauty sleep. Think about the sacrifice our daughter is making for us."

On and on they would go. Sometimes Seneca wondered how the two of them ever fell in love. They certainly worked well together as a team, keeping the house in order and ensuring she had everything she needed to train. But they were so different in so many ways. After nearly two decades together they rarely showed affection besides the odd hug or peck on the cheek.

It would take a special occasion for their lips to touch.

"Let's get started," she said, anxious to get the first step out of the way so she could move onto her favourite step.

The Obstacle Course.

Only elite athletes could maneuver their way through it without falling to the alligators below. Marie had created a course over the pond on the northwest corner of the Ellis-Brant property. They owned four acres, thanks to Catherine hiding some jewelry under her skirt when she was banished from Light City.

As punishment for choosing to love someone from The Darkness, a person from Light City was shamed by their peers and forced through the main gates with nothing but the clothes on their back.

Mama C had managed to walk out with a few extras.

Catherine typically quizzed Seneca on the first step for fifteen minutes. Today, they decided to double it to half an hour. After all, she was getting tomorrow off for her sixteenth birthday.

They began with the Ten Crow Convictions. Seneca rhymed them off easily, starting with, 'Thou shalt not worship any other God before the God of Light', and ending with, 'Thou shalt not disobey the Ten Crow Convictions'.

"And what happens to someone who is disobedient?"

"All offenders shall be permanently removed from Light City."

After that, they tackled the basic principles. There was no time to go over all of them, so her mother quizzed her randomly on the thousands of laws that governed Light City.

"Who has the right to bear arms?"

"Officers with the Barsicon Police Force, and the Northern Warriors who make up the Crow Corps," Seneca answered automatically.

"Any other citizen found in possession of a weapon will be..."

"...banished to The Darkness."

"And if they use that weapon to cause harm?"

"The sentence is death."

Rules, rules and more rules. The half hour flew by. Before long, Marie showed up to collect Seneca from the garden.

"Let's hit the course. I hope you stretched this morning."

CHAPTER 8

THE OBSTACLE COURSE

The obstacle course Marie constructed over the pond was a replica of the one used during the Light Ceremonies. Minus the alligators. Every dimension was a near duplicate. From the swinging v-rings to the towering cargo net Seneca would need to scale to reach the third step.

"This has always been my favourite part, Ma."

"I'm well aware. You're going to clear that course in record time on Saturday."

"That's the plan!"

The swinging v-rings were the first of seven obstacles. Seven rings attached to the end of seven swinging chains. They were shaped in an upside down 'V'. Four rings led to the top. Three would carry her down.

After the swinging v-rings was the barrel run. One wrong step along the seven wooden cylinders and a Light Seeker was in the water with the underfed alligators.

Seneca knew exactly where she needed to step and how fast she needed to run to fly across the barrels. Quick, light steps. Right down the middle. Otherwise, the barrel would start spinning. If that happened, unless a person possessed incredible grip and core strength, their odds of recovering were slim.

Quick movements were also necessary to get past the third obstacle on the course.

The gauntlet of spikes.

Seneca would have to manipulate her body through a narrow passageway with random spikes protruding from the walls. Running through it was not an option. Each movement had to be calculated. Jumps, ducks and side steps were necessary to reach the end.

There was zero room for error.

For the final four obstacles she had to clear the collapsing monkey bars and balance her way across a tightrope. Then climb up a seven-storey cargo net and slide down a metal pole onto the third step.

"Watch yourself on those barrels. It may seem like a breeze but take no obstacle for granted."

"Got it, Ma!"

Seneca jumped onto the platform at the edge of the pond and grabbed hold of the first ring with both hands. She took a step back to build momentum, then easily swung up to the second ring, flexing her biceps to gain height.

It took no time to get to the top and less time to get back down.

With the swinging v-rings out of the way, she sprinted towards the rolling barrels.

"Remember to stay in the middle," Marie yelled from the grass. "Move swiftly."

"Don't blink or you might miss it," Seneca laughed and took off at full speed.

This was a fun run for her.

Having cleared the rolling barrels, she headed toward the gauntlet of spikes. If she reached out, she could touch both walls in the seven-metre-long lane.

The number seven came up many times during a Light Seeker's journey through the Seven Steps into the Light. That must be on purpose. Seven obstacles. Seven rings. Seven barrels. Gauntlets and tightropes that were seven-metres long and cargo nets seven-storeys high.

No way that was a coincidence.

The only difference between their replica of the gauntlet of spikes and the real thing were the actual spikes themselves. Ma had fashioned homemade skewers out of wood and foam, then spray-painted them silver for a metallic look.

They couldn't risk impaling her during training.

Seneca jumped to fend off jabs at her ankles, dropped to the ground to escape upper body hits and arched her back to avoid being gutted. Would she be able to keep her cool when the spikes were real?

Of course.

This was her destiny.

The collapsing monkey bars were next. Seven bars each spread one metre apart. Light Seekers were given a mere two seconds from the time they touched the bar until it gave way. Taking a backswing was next to impossible. Most Light Seekers who attempted it turned into alligator soup.

Seneca loved the monkey bars. An airy feeling carried her from rung to rung. It was fiercely freeing to soar through the sky after making it through the gauntlet of spikes.

Monkey bars out of the way, she crossed the tightrope.

Most people couldn't even stand on a tightrope, let alone take a few steps without falling. Seneca was as steady as an ant walking down a highway.

Then it was up the cargo net and down the pole.

"Great job, Sen!"

"Thanks. It felt good."

"Keep moving that quickly and you'll beat Mama C back to the house."

"Good," she replied, sarcastically. "It's about time I was given a breather between steps."

Marie's expression grew serious. "You won't get a breather on Saturday night."

She removed her foot from her mouth. "You're right, Ma. I'm sorry."

Today was not the day for jokes. Seneca could see her mother was barely holding it together. Calm, cool, collected Marie was on edge.

"I'll run up to the house. If Mama's not back yet, I'll get started without her."

She sprinted towards their log cabin, blinking rapidly to slow the tears.

"Dear God of Light, please help me make it through this day with my sanity intact," she prayed, but received no reassurance from up above.

CHAPTER 9

THE MIND CHALLENGE

"The mind is a powerful thing," Catherine launched into her spiel, repeating the same words President Crow would recite two days from now.

"On the third step, we will challenge your knowledge. Seven questions. Each one will be harder than its predecessor. Light Seeker, are you prepared to prove your mental superiority?"

"I am, Madam President."

"We shall proceed."

The training questions were different each day. They tested Seneca's knowledge in areas such as math, history, science, language and geography. Light Seekers were expected to solve complex math problems and recall events from the past, right down to the day of the week they happened.

Luckily, she had the mind of a steel trap.

Her moms thought she had an eidetic memory, but she believed she simply loved to learn.

Seneca found comfort in the volumes of encyclopedias, classic novels and math textbooks she studied. Curiosity always got the best of her. She would start researching a topic after lunch in their home library and lose complete track of time. Hours would pass without her realizing it, until her moms called her for dinner.

Several jokes were made about breaking down the wall between Seneca's bedroom and the library. That way she wouldn't have to sneak in at night to read.

On more than one occasion, Catherine had discovered her fast asleep on the green shag carpet beneath the bookshelves.

"Sleep is just as important for your brain as learning," she would tell her.

Heavy footsteps on the porch startled both women.

"Well, hello there! How are my favourite gals?" JD shouted through the screen door.

For a man who trained others to sneak up quietly on the enemy, he certainly made a lot of noise.

"Come on in. Just finishing up," said Catherine. "Cup of tea? Glass of orange juice?"

"Thank you, but no thank you. No break time on final training day! We have two hours before my cousin arrives. By the way Catherine, would it be okay if I brought Alex to Seneca's birthday party tomorrow?"

Catherine hesitated and JD jumped back in. "Unless it's a problem. If it's a matter of food, I can bring along some extra chicken and eggs."

A stranger at her birthday party? How cool would that be! She was never allowed to meet anyone new unless it was approved by her moms. They had to keep her as focused as possible. Introducing her to anyone who could steer her off the path wasn't permitted.

"No problem at all. There's plenty of food to go around," Catherine said. "Alex is welcome to join us."

A surge of joy. No training tomorrow. Plus, birthday celebrations that included all her loved ones *and* a stranger! JD was an intriguing person. She could only imagine how interesting his cousin would be.

Then reality struck.

Tomorrow could be her second last day on Earth.

Moments ago, her stomach had been filled with excited butterflies. Now it was full of angry moths. Seneca imagined a single moth blinded after the light went out. Would her light go out on Saturday night?

Not if she could help it.

She hadn't spent her entire life training to be a Light Seeker only to be overcome by fear now.

JD held open the door for her.

"Are you ready?" he asked.

"So ready," she replied, and she meant it.

After all, even a blinded moth eventually regains its sight.

CHAPTER 10

FIGHT A WARRIOR

Combat training took place on a concrete slab. The same hard flooring on which Seneca would battle a Northern Warrior. Too bad she couldn't fight an officer from the Barsicon Police Force. It would be over a lot quicker.

The BPF consisted of 25,000 men and women who responded to minor incidents. The 'Bylaw Peacekeepers Force' is how most people referred to them. A noise complaint at ten o'clock in the morning and an officer from the BPF was there to deal with it.

However, serious law and order in Barsicon was handled by the Northern Warriors. The Crow Corp. 40,000 strong and all men.

Massive men.

Battling a Northern Warrior took more brains than brawn. When it came to brawn, the battle was already won.

The warriors stood 10-feet tall. To Seneca, they appeared just as wide. The hair on their heads grew out of their chins. Tattoos covered their scalps.

All the Northern Warriors sported long goatees, held in place by gold-coloured rings. One ring contained the hair directly at the chin and more were added every four inches or so. Some of the older warriors had twelve or thirteen rings on their beards. Those were the ones Seneca prayed she wouldn't have to fight.

When it came to the Northern Warriors, old did not mean weak.

While a wall separated Light City from The Darkness, it was a massive forest that divided the north from the rest of Barsicon. A border of trees. Those who snuck past the border and stepped into the Northern Forest, never stepped out again.

According to the history books Seneca had studied, the Northern Warriors were brought in following the Battle of Barsicon to ensure there would never be another toppling of the throne. Many of them fought to save the people of Barsicon during a military coup back in 1972. The one-day attack claimed the lives of King Quinton and Queen Raya, and likely their daughter Mildred, who disappeared that day and was never seen again.

At the time, Walter Crow was head of the Royal Privy Council and had no real power. Until he killed General Homer Thomson during a takeover at the castle, saved young Matilda and somehow managed to convince a large number of Northern Warriors to cross the border to fight in defense of Barsicon. Real power came swiftly after that.

The warriors replaced the military and Walter Crow was their leader.

For reasons unknown to Seneca, Walter demanded to be called 'General' after the battle of '72, despite the fact that he was not one. He was elected president after the failed coup. Became King in 1979 when he married Matilda, who was not quite fourteen at the time. But he never earned the title of General. He simply assigned it to himself and no one was brave enough to dispute it.

Questioning General Walter Crow was off the table. Unless you were prepared to have your door, and teeth, kicked in by a giant with a ringed beard.

Some believed the warriors were genetically modified. Others simply said they, "Grew em' big in the north". Either way, the warriors continued to multiply even though their wives and children were never seen.

Some tall tales claimed the warriors were robots and had no wives or children. Seneca quickly dismissed that theory. Warriors bled. That was proven on the fourth step.

Others believed the warriors had tiny wives, who only lived long enough to birth massive children. Hence the reason only men served in the Crow Corps.

Another popular legend was that the women were even larger than the men and it was those large ladies who would one day come down from the north, open the borders and demand real peace in Barsicon.

That was her favourite version.

Seneca often pondered why the fourth step wasn't called 'Kill A Warrior', since that's what she would have to do to complete it.

When a Light Seeker stepped up to fight, it was a fight to the death.

Kill or be killed.

They reached the fight pad and JD removed his shirt, showing off his scar-filled torso. The discoloured lines were the only thing that distracted the eye from his spiky purple and pink mohawk. He was toned, not bulky, and much stronger than he appeared at first glance.

Seneca removed her shoes and stepped onto the warm concrete. Shoes were never worn during a Light Ceremony, so she learned to fight in bare feet. It hurt at first. Eventually, the bottoms of her feet were as hard as the soles of her shoes.

"Okay, let's get started!" said JD, and they took their places. "We'll begin by reviewing the best techniques for taking down a large opponent. Then we'll go over pressure points you can use to weaken or completely impair them. Before we finish, we'll brush up on the best ways to escape an enemy hold."

"Yes, sir!"

For the next two hours, they grappled and sparred in the hot sun. Seneca was on top of her game. She held her own against JD, deflecting his attacks and setting him up for the kill on several occasions.

The kill.

Would she be able to take a human life when it came down to it? Keep squeezing past their last breath? She had the physical and mental strength to twist a warrior's head fast enough to snap his neck. The real question was whether she had the emotional strength to go through with it.

JD did his best to teach her how that might feel.

"Ready to go kill our lunch?" he asked, their thoughts aligned.

"I do love the taste of a good chicken."

Seneca left her shoes beside the concrete pad and headed across the lawn to JD's house. The grass was a welcome relief on her sore feet, cooling her extremities with each step as she headed in the direction of the chicken coop.

"Not today." JD motioned towards the house. "Come with me."

"But I thought we were getting a chicken to kill for lunch?"

JD's messy bungalow was once a trailer. Until the day he parked it next to Marie's toolbox. It wasn't dirty, just messy. He cleaned regularly around piles of clothes, books, weapons and tech items he loved to tinker with. If JD wasn't practicing martial arts or reading, he was fixing up old televisions and radios.

JD was a man with connections who liked to stay connected.

Computers were not allowed in The Darkness. Still, he had managed to get his hands on a few over the years. He stashed them beneath his house in a secret bunker Marie had built into the extension.

Her moms were furious when they discovered he had shown her the hidden room.

"Have you lost your mind?! I can't believe you let her go down there," they berated him.

Seneca was almost certain her moms hadn't been as upset about her seeing the computers as they had been about her viewing the huge cache of weapons that were not-so hidden away.

Always running around amidst the chaos was Cooper, JD's pet chicken. At nine years old, he was technically a rooster, but JD ignored her when she told him that.

"He will always be my 'pet poulet', Seneca."

Despite his age, Cooper showed no signs of slowing down. Every day, he would wait at the door for JD to come home. JD would pat him on the head and ask, "Is Cooper feeling all cooped up?" Then he would set him loose to roam the yard.

Seneca took comfort in the routine. She hopped up the steps behind JD, ready to give Cooper her own little pat.

She was going to miss him.

As expected, Cooper was waiting at the door when they arrived. Ready to receive affection and anxious to explore. His daily walks had become a taunt to all the other birds confined to the chicken coop. Seneca wasn't sure if a rooster could prance but that's what Cooper appeared to do on his jaunts around the yard. Proud as a peacock as he strutted his stuff. It seemed as though he lived for his walks.

Perhaps that was the secret to his longevity.

JD opened the screen door and bent down towards Cooper. Instead of patting him on the head, making his usual joke about being 'all cooped up', he picked up his pet and handed him to her.

"Cervical dislocation will be the method today."

"Very funny, JD!" she laughed and gave the rooster a mini rubdown. "He's such a joker. Isn't he, Cooper?"

Seneca kissed the bird on the head and looked up at JD with a smile.

The smile wasn't returned.

"You're kidding me, right?" she asked, instantly horrified at the possibility that he was not.

"No, no joke. Taking a human life will not be easy, Seneca. There is a different feeling attached to it. A feeling you must accept and overcome if you wish to fulfill your destiny."

"So you want me to kill Cooper? Just snap his neck, no big deal and then what? We eat him for lunch? This is messed up, JD."

"It's the only way. Do you trust me?"

"Of course."

"You have killed many of my birds before today."

"We both know this is different."

Did she spot a brief look of acknowledgement in his eyes before JD's expression faded blank?

"Treat it no differently."

Seneca moved quickly. Holding Cooper in her left arm, she used her right hand to grab onto the area where his skull met his neck and snapped it with a forceful movement.

Down and out.

JD eyed her closely and waited for a reaction.

Accept and move forward, accept and move forward, she repeated to herself. That's what one must do to survive.

"Time for baptism practice. Catherine is waiting by the pond for you." JD casually took Cooper's carcass from her hands. "I'll see you at lunch."

She ran at top speed towards the pond to practice holding her breath, the lump in her throat already making it hard to breathe.

CHAPTER 11

BAPTISM PRACTICE

"Breathe all the way in. Now let go. Don't fully exhale, just let go. Good, again. Breathe all the way in and let go."

Catherine took Seneca through breathing exercises to prepare her for the fifth step. To say she was nervous about this particular step would be an understatement. Every time she thought about it, a wave of anxiety crashed against her chest.

"Again. Five more times. Breathe all the way in. Now let go. Don't push the breath out, simply let go. Good, again. All the way in."

Mama C's voice was soothing. Even when Seneca went through the ritual alone, sometimes several times a day, it was Catherine's voice she heard in her head.

"Last time. Deep breath. All the way in. GO!"

A peaceful feeling washed over Seneca as she lowered herself into the pond. Her heartbeat naturally slowed. Her mind instantly entered a meditative state. The first few minutes of baptism practice were usually relaxing.

Even stale pond water seemed refreshing after fight training.

Catherine sat on her baptism bench. The wrought-iron seat was created with built-in storage for Mama C's chalkboard. For years, she used the erasable square to write down target times.

Target times and breathing techniques weren't used in the beginning. Back before the baptism bench was built by none other than the magnificent Marie, Catherine would sit in the shallows and tell Seneca to take a deep breath in, go underwater and hold it.

That was the extent of her training.

"Stay underwater just a bit longer today. You can do it, baby!" she would hear Catherine shout.

The words of encouragement muffled by Seneca's subaqueous skull.

Pleasing her mother had been difficult back then. If she held her breath for less than two minutes, even at four or five years old, she could tell Catherine was displeased. Around the age of eight, when she started to hold her breath for three minutes with incredible ease, she assumed Mama C would relax a little.

Not so.

They were both riddled with anxiety daily. Until Marie made a suggestion that changed the way they trained forever.

"Instead of panicking and always holding your breath until you nearly pass out each day, never knowing if it will be enough, why don't you set a goal to reach. Feel good about the outcome every now and then. While you're at it, maybe learn a few of those breathing techniques JD mentioned yesterday at lunch."

That's when the real baptism training started and when target times came into play.

Catherine would write down a time on her handheld chalkboard. When Seneca hit the target, she was allowed to come up for air. A tug at the rope around her waist signaled her success.

The rope was used in her baptism training until she turned fourteen. It was a constant reminder of the day she'd held her breath too long and Catherine had to fish her out of the pond.

"Don't you ever scare *me* like that again!" she'd lectured Seneca, both hands over her own heart while her daughter gasped for air.

With Catherine, it was always about Catherine.

At first, there seemed to be no rhyme or reason for the target times she picked. Then Seneca learned the truth. Searching for a shirt in her parents' closet, she stumbled upon records detailing the

Light Ceremonies of many past Light Seekers. Their names, ages and what steps they died on.

Among the information was a separate list of Light Seekers who died during their baptism and the length of time they were able to stay under before they drowned.

Catherine had been using those exact times as targets.

Finally, she understood why Mama C would get so upset on the days she didn't succeed.

Marie was enraged when she found out and came up with a new system. That night after dinner, they all sat down and wrote out target times on scraps of paper. The times went into a bucket they carried to the pond each day for six months, until Catherine got tired of lugging it around and promised to come up with random numbers.

Now they were two days away from the real thing and there were no more ropes.

No more target times.

Unable to hold her breath any longer, Seneca counted to thirty before she resurfaced. The mind can always force the body to go a bit further.

Today's time could be a new record.

"Ma...Mama. D...di...did I...do it?"

Catherine still used her chalkboard to display the length of time Seneca had held her breath. The chalk numbers should be higher than seven minutes. The longest she'd been under before today was six minutes and forty-seven seconds.

She watched Catherine write the numbers down while she regained control of her airway. Her mom had a huge smile on her face, as she turned the chalkboard around one last time.

It read: 7:54.

Was she seeing that correctly?

Yes, she had held her breath for almost eight minutes!

The longest time ever recorded for a baptism was just over twelve minutes and the Light Seeker had drowned before the seven-minute mark.

The records Seneca discovered confirmed the exact time. Although she didn't need records to recall that Light Ceremony from a decade ago. She had witnessed it.

The Light Seeker had been smart and strong. Everyone expected her to make it into Light City. She had also been promiscuous, according to whispers in The Darkness after she drowned.

"Seems Louise's lungs couldn't handle the ol' soul cleansin'," a woman had said.

"Probably took most of that time to clean between her legs," one man quipped and they all laughed.

After overhearing the chatter, Seneca had asked her moms to explain the definition of promiscuous.

"I've never heard that word before. What does it mean? Why did that woman's soul cleansing take so long?"

"Dirty souls take longer to clean," Catherine had told her, and that was that.

Seneca vowed to stay as pure as possible from that day forward.

Whatever that meant.

CHAPTER 12

PLEAD YOUR CASE

On the sixth step Light Seekers were given 500 words or less to plead their case. The observant ones recognized that President Barbara Crow became annoyed after the first 300 words. Being precise was key.

Relaying a message she wanted to hear, absolutely critical.

Every Saturday night, as far back as Seneca could remember, she watched her mothers write furiously on their notepads. Their records included every reason a Light Seeker gave for why they should be allowed into Light City, and whether they were granted access on the seventh step.

The God of Light's Final Judgement.

White smoke and the glass box opened. The clouds parted. A ray of sunshine beamed down and the Light Seeker was invited to step into the light.

Black smoke and they simply vanished. Ashes to ashes. Dust to dust.

But before they could even think about stepping into the glass box, a Light Seeker had to plead their case.

"I'm extremely handsome. Surely there are some beautiful women in the city looking for a guy just like me."

Black smoke.

"Getting into Light City would be a dream for me and my son. It's just the two of us. I'm a lawyer and my little Mikey-G is a star soccer player in The Darkness."

White smoke.

"Please, President Crow. I beg of you. My family of eight is starving in The Darkness. My wife can't work because of chronic pain and we have two sets of triplets under six years old."

Black smoke.

"I know it's a privilege and not a right to live in Light City."

White smoke.

Black.

White.

Black.

White.

The two hues dominated Seneca's sleep. White smoke overwhelmed her dreams. Black smoke engulfed her nightmares.

Just then, Marie approached them from behind and threw her arms across the back of the baptism bench.

"Let's do this one more time," she said.

"Can I play President Crow today and you can plead my case to me?"

"Nice try, little lady. Let's go."

They didn't have far to go. Thirty feet from the pond was one of Marie's easier construction projects. A replica of the sixth step.

The wooden podium had two steps leading up to it and sat in the middle of a cement pad. Seneca would have to kneel on the hard ground to plead her case.

"Welcome Light Seeker to the sixth step. During the seventh and final step you will face the ultimate judgement, with the God of Light determining your fate."

Destiny.

"As the leader of Light City, I too shall have a say. My job is to determine whether allowing you and your family to reside here is in the best interest of the people. Once you have finished, I will confer with the God of Light while you make your way to the glass box and await your final judgement. You may now plead your case."

The next 300 words had been carefully crafted over the years. Her short speech had made it through multiple revisions, and Seneca delivered each word clearly and effectively.

When she was done, Marie stepped down from the podium and helped her to her feet. "You were incredible today."

"Thank you for everything, Ma. The only reason I am about to fulfill my destiny is because of you and Mama C. I promise to make you so proud."

They hugged. Tears spilled down Marie's cheeks and landed in Seneca's hair, neither in a hurry to end their embrace.

"You've already made us so proud." Marie placed her palms over Seneca's cheeks and planted a kiss on her forehead. "You are going to be a successful Light Seeker. There is no doubt in my mind."

If only she could say the same.

CHAPTER 13

SENECA MEETS ALEX

"Sen! Can you run over to JD's and borrow a cup of flour?"

"Sure, Mama C. Just one cup?"

"That should do it. Thanks. I must've used all of ours when I baked your birthday cake."

Light training was over.

Forever.

What a strange sensation.

Seneca had spent the afternoon sailing Fee Fee down the Fennell River with Marie. Catherine stayed back to prepare dinner. Chicken was on the menu that night and Seneca double checked to make sure it had come from the freezer.

Poor Cooper.

She still had a hard time coming to grips with the fact that she had murdered him just hours before. The innocent bird was expecting a love pat and received a death snap-of-the-neck instead.

JD would probably serve him up without batting an eye.

Is that what made him an ultimate warrior?

Leaving her shoes behind, Seneca jumped over the porch steps and took off to JD's. Despite her busy day, she still had enough energy to sprint the entire way. When she reached the door, she stuck her foot out instinctively to stop Cooper from trying to escape.

Sigh.

"Hello, JD? I need to borrow some flour. Mind if I just grab---"

Seneca's body slammed into someone who was definitely not JD.

AH!

Aaaaaaaahhhhh!!!

Two screams. Only one came from her.

"Sorry to scare you," they threw their hands up. "I'm Alex. Jamie's cousin."

Seneca had never heard anyone call him Jamie before. "That's okay. It's my fault. I was the one who came barging in."

Alex shared the same ebony skin as JD, but not the same hairdresser. No brightly-coloured mohawk. Short hair instead, and mesmerizing cat-like eyes. They were brown with flecks of gold. Or were they gold with flecks of brown? It was hard to tell. Seneca couldn't look away.

"It's a pleasure to meet you," said Alex.

Seneca blushed and blurted, "I'm never allowed to meet new people."

What was wrong with her? Why did she say that? Probably because she was never allowed to meet new people. Her palms were suddenly slick with sweat. Her heart raced. She was consumed by the energy being emitted from the person in front of her.

Alex's voice was as smooth as the silk outfit they wore; a baggy button-up shirt and matching pants, splashed with yellows, greens and oranges...actual oranges.

When they spoke, her heart skipped a beat. "My cousin has told me a lot about you. Big birthday tomorrow. Sixteen?"

"Ye...yeah."

"I still remember my sixteenth birthday party. Of course, it would be terrible if I didn't. It was only two years ago. Two years ago *today* actually."

"Today is your birthday?"

"It is. Number eighteen for me. Guess I'm officially an adult now."

Without hesitation, she threw herself into Alex's arms for a hug. "Happy Birthday!"

The hug was reciprocated. It was a first that felt familiar. As if they had hugged thousands of times before. Seneca rested her head on Alex's shoulder and inhaled a pleasant new scent.

A loud clang eventually pulled her away.

Now it was time for Alex to blush. "I think that might be the best birthday hug I've ever received."

"Thank you," she said. "I mean, you're welcome. Wait, you didn't say thank you."

Alex laughed. "Thank you."

The clanging started again. Through the window, she could see JD digging a hole. His shovel hit rock several times as he poked around looking for a spot.

A spot for what?

"Can I get that cup of flour for you?" asked Alex, reminding her why she was there in the first place.

"Yes, please. I'm just going to check in with JD. Be right back."

Seneca found him in the backyard under a tall dawn redwood. With his perfect spot located, he was now digging for depth. Seneca's arrival had gone unnoticed. Dirt flew from JD's shovel onto her bare feet.

"Whoa! Watch it."

This time he stopped in mid-swing. The dirt continued. With less momentum, it landed in front of her toes instead of on top of them.

"Sorry, Seneca. I didn't see you there."

That was when she noticed the brown sack. It was barely big enough to hold Cooper's body. The rooster's head protruded out the top at an awkward angle. Her doing. But why was he burying the bird? JD always ate the meat he killed.

Or the meat she killed.

He had handed Cooper over for slaughter without hesitation. Now he was out here digging a grave. It didn't make sense.

"I came over to borrow a cup of flour." Seneca pointed at the brown sack. "Is that Cooper?"

JD answered with a quick nod and continued digging, throwing the dirt in the opposite direction this time.

"But I just assumed we would---"

"We would what?" he laughed. "Eat him at your birthday party tomorrow?"

Seneca couldn't tell if JD was joking.

He stopped digging and leaned on his shovel. "In life, we must respect the purpose of all living things. We must honour our spiritual and emotional connections. That is different for everyone."

Another one of JD's lessons was coming her way. She could tell by the way he looked through her. On his forehead, she counted ten newly formed wrinkles between his eyebrows and his neon mohawk.

"Think of it this way, Seneca. You are willing to kill a human being on Saturday night to become a Light Seeker. Correct?"

"Well...yes."

"Would you kill your Ma Marie or Mama C to get into Light City?"

"No. Of course not!"

"Because you are connected to them. You love them. Not only will you kill for them, you will die for them."

"Anyone would kill for someone they love," said Seneca.

JD shook his head. "Not true."

"What do you mean?"

"Some people feel connected to all living things. They would not kill. Regardless of the situation. In fact, some risk their own lives to protect all living things. You hear about them in the news. Those people who chain themselves to trees to try and save them from being cut down. They know there's a good chance the Northern Warriors will slice them to pieces with their mighty machines, wipe them out along with the old oak trees, and they do it anyway."

"So they have empathy for all living things and I don't? Is there something wrong with me?"

"No, Seneca. You're wired with the traits you need to fulfill your destiny."

"Killing Cooper made me sad. Normally I have no problem killing your chickens. Today was different."

"Because you had an emotional attachment to him. Which is exactly why I am digging a hole right now."

JD went back to slinging dirt over his shoulder. Seneca looked down at the brown sack. Stared into Cooper's blank eyes. Killing her feathery friend had made her queasy. Still, she had gone through with it, as she would with any task that got her closer to her ultimate goal.

"What would you have done with Cooper if I wasn't emotionally attached to him? You loved him too. Would you still be burying him?"

He stopped digging for good this time and stabbed his shovel into the dirt pile. "If you weren't attached to this bird, I would be saucing him up and throwing him on the grill tonight."

JD tossed the brown sack into the hole in the ground and started the burial process. The dirt pile disappeared, as the soil was returned to its place.

Seneca stood by in disbelief. "Eat him? You can't be serious, JD."

"Sure, I can. Would you die for a tree?"

"No, that's ridiculous."

"Why? Because you can't connect emotionally with a tree? Well, I can't connect emotionally with a chicken. Like I said, we are all blessed with the traits we need to fulfill our destiny. On the flip side, the Creator also withholds certain characteristics that would only impede us on our journey. Can you imagine me being an empathetic person?"

"But you are empathetic. You're burying a chicken for me!"

"It has nothing to do with the chicken. It's because I have sympathy for you," JD explained. "I could see that it bothered you to kill Cooper, so I just assumed you wouldn't want anyone to eat him. I'm not an empath, Seneca. *Or* a psychopath!"

They both laughed. "In all honesty, I was horrified at the thought of having him for dinner."

"Oh, you poor girl. I would never do that to you!" JD paused. "Before we go, do you want to say a few words?"

"I wouldn't know what to say."

"Whatever comes to mind."

Seneca stared down at the tampered ground and started her eulogy. "Blessings to the God of Light for creating Cooper, the magnificent bird who lived a long life and served a great purpose. I'll miss watching you strut around the yard. Thanks for teaching me something new about life and about myself. I'm forever grateful."

"That was beautiful, Seneca. Now, let's head back for that cup of flour."

"Don't you want to say anything, JD?"

He paused. "Uh, sure. I don't see why not."

Following Seneca's lead, he looked down at the pile of dirt to say his final farewell. "My dear pet poulet. What can I say? You loved to eat. You loved to poop. You've finally flown Earth's chicken coop."

"JD!"

"Ha! You had no idea I was such a poet."

Arm in arm, giant grins plastered across their faces, they headed back to the house. Alex was waiting for them in the kitchen. A cup of flour was on the counter ready to go.

"Seneca, this is my cousin I was telling you about. Alex."

They replied in unison. "We've met."

All three laughed.

"I didn't see you in the backyard, so I came in the house and ran into Alex---"

"Literally ran into me," added Alex.

A rush of heat surged through her body when she thought about the hug they had shared. Worried JD would see her blush, she turned to Alex. Unfortunately, that only made her face turn a brighter shade of red.

"I should get back with that flour before Mama C starts to worry."

Catherine's voice rang out in the distance. "Seneca Ellis-Brant!"

Why did she always have to yell out her full name? Embarrassed, Seneca grabbed the cup of flour from the counter and turned to leave. As she did, her shoulder brushed up against Alex's arm. A burst of energy, like an electric shock, flowed through her entire body. She'd never been so physically affected by someone's sheer presence or slight touch.

"Thanks for the flour. I guess I'll see you both at my party tomorrow?"

"We'll see you before then," said JD. "Marie asked me to stop by and listen to you ladies rehearse a song for the party. I figured since Alex is a singer, it only makes sense that my dear cousin should join us."

"You're a singer? Cool!"

JD looked at his cousin with pride. "Alex has a regular gig at one of those luxurious nightclubs in Light City. What's it called again?"

"Lupia's."

"Yes! That's it, Lupia's. R&B, jazz, you name it. You should take your moms there next week after you've settled in."

Catherine called out louder this time. "Seneca Ellis-Brant!!!"

"Better run. See you after dinner."

The return trip home was slower. If she took off at full speed, she wouldn't make it back with a full cup of flour. She jogged across the fight pad, past the pond and up the steps, onto the porch that wrapped around their entire log cabin. This time, she accidentally slammed the screen door behind her.

Catherine was not amused. "Be careful. You almost pulled the door right off the hinges!"

"Sorry, Mama C. It won't happen again." Seneca set the white dust down on the counter beside her mother. "I have the flour for you."

Catherine had been cooking for hours, yet somehow resembled a model about to walk the runway. Bright, red lips matched her high heels. The shoes were elegant, though scuffed around the edges. Her black, sleeveless dress pulled tight at the waist and puffed at the knees, aided by a crinoline skirt. The dress came dangerously low in the front and the back. Catherine's black and white pinstripe apron only added to the outfit's appeal.

"What took you so long?"

"I met Alex."

"Oh, that's right. JD's cousin arrived today."

"They're stopping in later tonight to listen to us rehearse for the party. Ma asked them to come by. Have we decided which song we're going to play?"

Catherine looked perturbed.

"What's wrong, Mama?"

Her mother brightened instantly, shook her head and smiled. "Nothing, honey. I just realized we haven't decided on a song yet. Silly us! Why don't you go look through the music book and pick out your favourite tune? It is *your* birthday after all."

Catherine's smile had wiped the concern from her face, but Seneca could still feel her mother's nervous energy. Was it because they were so close to the Light Ceremony and reality was starting to sink in? It certainly was for her. She could only imagine what it was like for her moms.

Especially Catherine.

Marie never disputed that Seneca should become a Light Seeker, but she also seemed content with their life in The Darkness. Catherine was another story. In an entirely different book, on a completely separate shelf, in a faraway library.

Seneca could tell Catherine yearned for her old lifestyle in Light City. Ached to go back to the place where she could wear brand new stilettos to a fancy restaurant. Dine at an establishment where the plates had no cracks. Where she was simply a patron. Not the chef, server and dishwasher as well. After the Light Ceremony on Saturday, that could be their new life.

That *would* be their new life.

By this time next week she would be dining at Lupia's. Watching Alex perform on a stage that she could only conjure up in her imagination. What was it about Alex that drew her in? She couldn't stop thinking about them. About how they made her feel when they spoke or touched her. It was unlike anything she had experienced before.

Seneca walked on air from the kitchen to the study, on the hunt for a perfect song. Her heart, already singing.

CHAPTER 14
LOG CABIN JAM

There was a chill in the air outside the log cabin. Inside, it was cozy. Marie had started a fire. Catherine served up cups of hot cocoa and Seneca added an extra gift to the pile of wrapped presents on the windowsill.

"Can we practice our song one more time from the top?" she asked her moms.

Palms and fingertips tapped the bongos. Seneca performed a solo groove for a few bars. Then Marie joined in. Her mother strummed the intro effortlessly on her old six-string guitar and Catherine started to sing.

"Ooooohhh, ooooohhh."

She anticipated a knock at the door, expecting JD and Alex to show up any minute. The thought of performing in front of a professional musician was nerve wracking.

Or was she anxious because it was Alex?

Earlier, she had picked a song with them in mind. A tune she had played with her moms for many years. The song was called 'Soul Meeting'. It was written by Reuben Ball-Koster, a famous folk musician from The Darkness.

We fell in love before we met
One fateful summer's day
Two souls reunited in the flesh
To laugh, to love, to stay

On my journey through The Darkness
It's your love that lights my way
Tomorrow's not promised to anyone
Darling, I promise to love you today

Catherine sang the last note. Their instruments faded. Applause rang out from the kitchen.

JD and Alex had slipped in unnoticed.

"Bravo! Bravo!" shouted JD. "A most fabulous performance!"

Seneca flushed. "How long have you been standing there?"

"Long enough to see there is some serious musical talent in this household." Alex turned to Catherine, genuinely impressed. "You have some pipes!"

"Oh my, thank you," she replied.

Mama C was holding her hand out for Alex to shake? Kiss? It was difficult to tell the way it hovered in the air, as if she were resting her hand on the head of someone standing in front of her who was a foot shorter.

"I'm Catherine, but everyone around here calls me Mama C."

"Pleasure to meet you, Mama C. I'm Alex."

They were still wearing the silk outfit covered in oranges. It still looked as good as it had earlier. Maybe even better. Seneca waited to see how they would react to her mom's floating phalanges. Alex grabbed Catherine's hand and pulled her close for two quick kisses. One on each cheek.

"Well then," Catherine giggled. "It looks like the pleasure is both of ours now."

Marie introduced herself. "JD has told us wonderful things about you. It's great to finally meet. Come, have a seat."

The conversation flowed. Hours passed without anyone checking the clock. They shared hilarious stories from their youth. JD juggled five oranges for an impressive amount of time before the fruit went flying across the living room. Everyone laughed when he pretended he couldn't find two of the oranges, which had fallen onto Alex's lap.

"What's this?" Catherine picked up a gift from the windowsill. "I didn't put this here."

"Wasn't me," replied Marie.

"It was me," Seneca admitted. "Today is Alex's birthday."

The present was wrapped in an old newspaper. It was the best she could do on such short notice. She had tied it together with a simple piece of white string. Seneca took the gift from Catherine and handed it to Alex, who appeared truly shocked at the kind gesture.

"For me? You didn't have to---"

"I wanted to. Please, open it."

Alex untied the string and set it aside. They were unnecessarily delicate with the newspaper, which Seneca threw into the fire as soon as it was removed.

"A book! This is great. I love to read."

It wasn't just any book. It was Seneca's all-time favourite. 'Under the Orange Tree' by Pam Martin. The book had been a gift from her moms on her thirteenth birthday and she had read it countless times.

The short story was about a dancer named Lise who was born into a world without music. People would laugh at her when she danced down the streets. She heard music in her head and her body moved in sync with the melody in her mind.

"That woman has lost it!" the townspeople would say.

Until one day, Lise decided it was time for them to hear the music as well.

The single mother of four gathered her children and gave each of them different instruments she had invented. For her oldest, a handheld drum fashioned from sheepskin. The middle children were given a pair of maracas and a tambourine. The youngest was presented with a metal triangle and a steel rod. Together, they learned how to recreate the sounds that filled Lise's mind and compelled her to move to the rhythm.

When she was satisfied with the song they arranged, she invited her neighbours to join them under the orange tree in the middle of town.

A large crowd gathered in the park, curious to see what the woman who had lost her mind had on her mind. But she spoke not a single word. Simply nodded for her children to begin.

On her cue, the children played their instruments while Lise danced. The people stood and stared, unsure of what to do. Then spontaneously, from the middle of the crowd, a man did something no one had done before.

He sang.

His angelic voice brought out the music in others, who hummed or moved their feet along to the beat.

The town was so full of music by the end of the book, bands and choirs started to assemble. They created more instruments. Musicians travelled with the dancers to perform in countries near and far, lifting spirits around the world.

"Wow, Seneca. You're going to give it away?" asked Catherine.

"That's your favourite book," added Marie.

"It is," replied Seneca. "I know it by heart and that is where I'll keep my copy. This one belongs to Alex now."

"Are you sure?" asked Alex. "It seems to have special significance to you."

"It does. That's why I want you to have it."

The room went silent. The strong connection between Seneca and Alex was felt by the others. Marie and Catherine looked nervous. JD appeared more amused than anything else.

"Thank you, Seneca." Alex held the book to their chest. "I'll cherish it."

"You're welcome. Happy birthday."

"Yes, happy birthday. What a night it's been. So great to meet you, Alex," said Catherine. "But it is getting late and tomorrow is another big day."

"It's not that late," Seneca protested.

Marie jumped in. "It's almost ten. We have a lot on the go tomorrow---"

"But we still haven't heard Alex sing!"

"I'll sing at your party tomorrow. I promise."

"Promise?"

"It's a date."

Red-faced and giddy, she said goodbye and goodnight.

CHAPTER 15

UNDER THE ORANGE TREE

Seneca brushed her teeth and changed into her pajamas. She climbed into bed but couldn't sleep. An hour spent tossing and turning was enough for her. Crawling out from beneath the covers, she slipped into a pair of jeans and a t-shirt, opened the door and peered down the hall. Light streamed from under her parents' bedroom door.

They were still awake.

Seneca opened her window and carefully removed the screen. Maybe some fresh air would tire her out.

Not likely.

How could she sleep when she couldn't stop thinking about Alex? Plus, the Light Ceremony was only two days away. That should be her main focus.

Not someone she just met.

So why did she see them every time she closed her eyes? Had they read the book yet? Maybe it was too childish for someone who was officially an adult.

"I loved the book."

Great. Now she was hearing Alex's voice in her head. Seneca continued down the path that led to the orange grove when she heard it again.

"Hey, Seneca. I read the book and I loved it."

It was Alex.

In the flesh.

"What are you doing out here?" she asked.

"I was going for a late night stroll and witnessed your daring escape from the window. Thought I'd come by and tell you how much I love my new favourite story."

"I was worried it might seem silly."

They stepped between two rows of orange trees. "Silly? No way! Silly would be the two of us dancing under the orange trees."

Alex grabbed Seneca's hands and swung her around in a circle. They swayed back and forth to a beat that neither could hear, but both could feel. The silent song slowed with the tempo of their bodies, which they held against one another. She started to hum the song 'Soul Meeting'.

This time, Alex sang the words.

We fell in love before we met
One fateful summer's day
Two souls reunited in the flesh
To laugh, to love, to stay

Goosebumps formed across the entire surface of her body. Seneca had never heard a more enchanting sound in her life. Mama C was a good singer, but she had nothing on them. Alex was born to sing.

On my journey through The Darkness
It's your love that lights my way
Tomorrow's not promised to anyone
Darling, I promise to love you today

It was Seneca's turn to applaud. "Wow, I'm speechless. Your voice is like nothing I've ever heard. You sing each note as if the note were its own song! Seriously, I'm speechless. I have chills everywhere. You're so good. No, not good. Good doesn't even begin to describe it. You're incredible. Amazing. Mind blowing---"

"For someone who is speechless, you don't seem at a loss for words."

"*A-ha.* True," she pointed to a lush patch of grass under an orange tree. "Shall we sit?"

"Absolutely."

The ground was soft. The air was crisp. The stars were plenty.

They leaned into the tree. Touching shoulders.

Both comfortably muted.

Alex was the first to break to the silence. "Are you excited about your party tomorrow?"

"So excited I can't sleep apparently."

"You'll doze off sooner or later."

"Hopefully sooner tonight and not later tomorrow in the middle of my birthday cake."

"*Ha!* That would be a memorable party. How many people are coming?"

"Not many. My moms, obviously. You and JD," she paused.

"That's everyone?"

"No, but almost. The Coyvilles will be there. Have you met them?"

"No, not yet. Are they the elderly couple that own the brick farmhouse on Jude Lake?"

"Yes! They are the sweetest people you will ever meet. Ernest turned eighty last fall and still works six days a week in the garage, tinkering away on old cars. He fixes up vehicles for people in The Darkness for a fraction of the actual cost. Just to help out."

"Ernest sounds like an incredible guy."

"He is, and Helen is an incredible gal. She'll be eighty next month and she can still stand on her head! Mama C hired her to teach me yoga. The way that woman bends her body. Let me tell you. It's something else."

"I can't wait to meet them."

That grin. She couldn't resist it. It changed the chemistry in her body.

Would this happen every time she met a new person? Please, no. Seneca could barely handle the duelling emotions she was experiencing now. Calm and nervous. Comfortably on edge. A feverish chill through her entire body. Was Alex feeling the same thing? Probably not. They had met several people before her. Surely this was nothing new for them.

Then all of a sudden, something entirely new for her.

Alex reached out, placed a hand on top of Seneca's and turned it over. They slid their fingers between hers.

The way lovers did.

Up until this moment, Seneca had only held hands with her moms. Their fingers had never intertwined like this.

Alex glanced down at their hold. "Is this okay?"

She gripped tighter. "More than okay."

"Seneca, I know we've just met but I'm very drawn to you. Is that too forward to say?"

"Not at all. I feel the same way."

"This is turning out to be a really great birthday for me."

"It's amazing how life can change in a day. To think that just yesterday I didn't even know you. Today we celebrated your birthday. Tomorrow we'll celebrate mine."

"And one day after that is your Light Ceremony."

She had always dreamed of the day when she would redeem her family. Complete all Seven Steps and walk through the gates of Light City. Now she was in no hurry for that day to arrive.

Feeling alive had never been her main mission in life. Her life was about staying alive. Survival. But in that moment, sitting under the orange tree with Alex, she felt more alive than ever. As she breathed in the night air and concentrated on Alex's soft touch, she was determined to be a successful Light Seeker.

Not just for her moms, for her as well.

And not just to avoid death, but to feel this alive again.

"Speaking of things changing in a day," Alex peered down at their watch. "It's midnight. Time for *me* to wish *you* a happy birthday."

"My sweet sixteen has arrived! Do you have anything for me?" she joked.

"I do, actually," Alex replied and leaned in for a kiss.

Seneca had never kissed anyone romantically. Their lips touched. Softly at first. Moving gently. Exploring. The tip of Alex's tongue ran across her upper lip. For some reason, she felt it the strongest in her groin. At first, she mimicked Alex's gentle movements. Then instinct took over and she kissed them with fervor.

"Why do I feel like I'm melting into the earth, Alex?"

"I'm right there with you, Seneca."

Their eyes never left each other as they moved from sitting to kneeling. She strived to understand the urges boiling within her. One thing she could fully comprehend was her desire to kiss Alex again.

She leaned in.

"It makes total sense that you are a Light Seeker. I can literally feel the light radiating off you."

Yes, Seneca was a Light Seeker. As such, she shouldn't place herself in situations where she could be tempted by earthly pleasures. Kissing someone was not the kiss of death. It wasn't against the rules. However, any other sexual acts were forbidden and could result in an extra-long baptism on Saturday night.

Thoughts of drowning killed the mood and Alex noticed. "Is everything okay?"

"Everything is amazing. It's just that I have to get back now. If my moms discover I'm gone, they'll send out a search party."

"The kind of party you want to avoid on your birthday. I get that."

Seneca could see Alex was disappointed and she didn't blame them. She was too. There was nowhere else in the world she would rather be.

"Maybe before I go...a kiss goodnight?"

Alex's spirits seemed to lift immediately. "That's a great idea."

The second kiss was even more explosive than the first.

As they walked back to the log cabin hand in hand, Seneca imagined a life filled with passion and happiness. Was it possible? Did she deserve that level of bliss?

She believed in her destiny, but she also knew anything could happen on Saturday night. Many Light Seekers before her were convinced of their destinies and had failed.

If the end was near, so be it.

All she wanted was to spend her final hours on Earth getting to know the beautiful person who was standing in front of her, replacing her window screen and wishing her sweet dreams.

"Goodnight, Seneca."

They touched hands through the window screen. The wire mesh was the only thing that stopped their fingers from interlocking again.

"Night night."

She waited until Alex was out of sight, then shut the curtains. Her pajamas were still on the floor where she had ditched them earlier. She pulled them on and was crawling back into bed when she heard arguing.

"You're unbelievable sometimes!"

"Keep your voice down, Catherine. You'll wake Seneca."

But she was already awake.

As the fighting down the hall intensified, her mood shifted from captivated by Alex to confused by her mothers' words.

"What if we've spent all this time and energy turning her into a Light Seeker, then come Saturday night, she survives all Seven Steps into the Light?"

"I don't know, Marie. We'll just have to cross that bridge if we get there."

CHAPTER 16

A PRIVATE CONVERSATION

Marie's frantic voice cut through the quiet log cabin like a knife through a cloud. "We shouldn't go through with it."

Seneca's head was swimming. Had Marie just said *what if she survives?*

"We have to. It's going to be difficult at first, dealing with the fallout after the Light Ceremony. But then we'll be on our way to---"

"Exactly, Catherine. To where?"

"Marie, now is not the time to consider backing out. This has been sixteen years in the making. Now you want to pull the trigger prematurely? That doesn't make a lot of sense. It sounds like you don't trust me."

"You saw the way she was with Alex tonight. Maybe she can live a normal life here in The Darkness. Make real connections with people instead of being a pawn."

"My daughter is not a pawn!"

Marie shushed her. "Keep your voice down."

Seneca strained to hear the rest of the conversation but couldn't make out their muffled words. She needed to get closer. Tossing her blanket to the side, she crawled out of bed. Tip-toed across the room---

Clunk!

Tripped up by a cord, her bedside lamp toppled over. Luckily, the lamp didn't break when it hit the ground. The noise, however, was enough to alert her moms.

Seneca carefully placed the lamp back on the nightstand and dove into bed. She pulled the blanket over her shoulders just as Marie opened the door.

"Hey Sen," she whispered. "Everything okay in here?"

She groaned and rolled over, pretending to sleep. Marie entered and hovered over her. Seneca felt a hand on her back. A kiss on her forehead.

"My sweet, sweet girl. I pray I never lose you."

Marie left. Seneca stared at the ceiling and replayed the conversation in her mind. What she could remember of it anyway. Why was she a pawn? What plan was Ma Marie trying to back out of? She had trained her entire life to be a Light Seeker. The ceremony was less than two days away.

Now this?

It was just like she had talked about with Alex.

So much had changed in one day.

Seneca treasured the moments they had spent together in the orange grove. Their conversation. Their shared dance. Their kisses. Reliving their magical evening was the only reason she was able to stop rehashing her parents' argument and finally doze off.

CHAPTER 17

SENECA'S SWEET SIXTEEN

Friday, July 8th, 2022

The sun was up hours before Seneca. Rarely one to sleep in, she had been exhausted when she finally managed to drift off.

Last night seemed like a dream. Had Alex kissed her? Were her moms really arguing? It was all so hazy, and by the time the mental fog lifted, she was mostly filled with excitement about her birthday party.

At breakfast, she devoured pancakes with fresh strawberries. Mid-morning, they ventured off on a family sail down the Fennell River. Marie had seemed distracted the entire time. She kept checking on supplies, which were far too many, and ensuring Fee Fee was operating in tip-top shape.

Catherine practically had to force her to sit down and eat some vegetables with the fresh hummus Seneca had whipped up that morning.

"Mmmmmm. The perfect amount of garlic!"

"Thanks, Ma."

"We should be getting back soon," said Catherine. "Our guests are arriving in less than two hours and I still have a few things to prepare."

Back at home, Catherine made a beeline for the kitchen. Seneca and Marie grabbed their ball-catching gloves and headed straight to the backyard. The afternoon sun warmed their skin but didn't scorch it, thanks to the layers of sunscreen Catherine had insisted they apply before *and* after their boating excursion.

Marie's first throw was too high. Seneca jumped several feet in the air trying to catch it. The ball hit the tip of her glove and sailed past.

"Sorry. It slipped."

Seneca chased after it. "We're playing catch. Not fetch!"

In one swift motion, she retrieved the ball from the ground and threw it back to her mother. Today would normally be a training day and she hadn't exerted much energy. If the backyard had walls, she would be bouncing off them.

Marie noticed. "Maybe we *should* be playing fetch. I'm not sure I can keep up with you today."

"It's hard for me to slow down. You know that," she giggled.

"Yes, I do. I also know that it's necessary for you to take it easy today. Save your energy for tomorrow."

"Sure thing, Ma."

Seneca debated on asking her mom about the conversation she'd overheard the previous night. Maybe she shouldn't. Besides, she was starting to question whether she had misheard or misinterpreted what was said. She pushed away the nagging feeling and focused on burning off some extra energy.

Before long, Catherine was calling them in to freshen up for the party. "Let's go, ladies. Time to get pretty!"

Mama C was the only one who cared about getting pretty. It was undeniable though, Seneca wanted to look good for Alex. Maybe 'pretty' wasn't exactly the word, but she wanted to appear presentable. Attractive even.

"Do you want to shower first?" asked Marie.

"Sure. I won't be long."

Wet lines massaged and rejuvenated her. Out of the shower, she brushed the long side of her hair and ran damp fingers through the short side. She wasn't sure what else to do besides her regular routine.

Her birthday outfit consisted of loose-fitting black cargo pants and a bright red crop top. The tiny shirt exposed her shoulders and midriff.

Catherine had passed the garment down to Seneca on her twelfth birthday.

"This is the shirt I was wearing when I was removed from Light City. I had hoped to wear it the day we walk back through the gates, but there's *no way* I'll fit into that thing ever again!"

Seneca had tried it on. She felt extremely self-conscious and removed the shirt immediately. At twelve, it had practically fallen off her.

Today it fit perfectly.

The crop top defined her strong waistline. It hugged her chest and showed off her athletic shoulders. She discovered it at the back of her closet last week and decided to wear it to her birthday party.

If Catherine couldn't don it as a symbol of redemption, Seneca would sport it on her behalf.

Mama C would likely become emotional when she saw her wearing it. Maybe it would be best to surprise her before their guests arrived. Marie was in the shower. That afforded them some one-on-one time.

She slipped down the hall. "So, what do you think?"

Catherine was admiring herself in their full-length mirror when she caught a glimpse of Seneca standing inside the doorway. Her jaw dropped. She turned away from her reflection in slow motion. By the time she came face-to-face with her daughter, her chin was resting on her chest.

"I'm speechless, Seneca. You're stunning! That shirt looks marvelous on you. Wow. Gorgeous. Unbelievably beautiful. I mean, look at you. Seriously. I'm speechless. You're absolutely radiant."

Seneca thought back to her own speechless moment with Alex the night before.

So that's where I get it from.

"You look just like me. With Marie's dark hair, bronze skin and almond-shaped eyes, yes. But other than that, you look *exactly* like me. Wow. Just wow."

She stared at her blonde, blue-eyed mother. Even though Catherine had given birth to her, Seneca bore a strong resemblance to Marie. Photographs of Marie as a child were interchangeable with her own baby pictures.

Seneca had also seen photos of Mama C during her pregnancy and the subsequent stretch marks that lined her torso.

She really was a perfect combination of the two women.

A miracle from the God of Light.

The story of her birth was always told on her birthday. Seneca assumed this year would be no exception. Would Alex believe the story of how she came to be?

It was pretty unbelievable.

"Let's get the picture boards out for the party. We have to tell the story of your miracle birth. It's a tradition."

Get out of my head, Mama C.

"Sure, I'll grab them. Are they still in the hall closet?"

"They should be. Toss them in the living room and I'll check to make sure they're in order after I finish up the dishes."

"I'm ready for the party. I can double-check the picture boards."

"I thought you were about to offer to do the dishes."

"Well, it is my birthday."

Her mother ran her fingers through the long side of Seneca's hair. "You really are stunning. I don't think I've ever seen you look as beautiful as you do today."

Seneca beamed.

"Now go grab those picture boards so we can reminisce about the days when you had long hair on both sides of your massive head."

"Excuse me?"

"No joke. Those first few years your noggin was *way* too big for your body."

"Mama C!"

"I'm just teasing! Kinda. Now get out of here and let me finish getting ready so I can wash those dishes before Ernest and ---"

They were interrupted by a knock at the door. Catherine peeked out the window to see their elderly neighbours waiting patiently on the porch.

"Why do they always show up fifteen minutes early?"

Seneca looked at the clock on the bedside table. "It's three on the dot. The party is scheduled for three."

"Everyone knows you're not supposed to show up on time. It's rude!"

"Some people think it's rude to be late."

Catherine waved her hand in the air. "Hogwash. Can you go let them in? I'm right behind you."

Seneca entertained Ernest and Helen for ten minutes before Catherine came in 'right behind' her. The clock read half past three by the time JD and Alex arrived. Having lived next door for many years, JD knew it was in his best interest *not* to show up on time. Unless it was for training. In that case, he better not be late.

Marie met them at the door and ushered them inside. "Come in, come in."

"JD, welcome to the party!" said Catherine. "And Alex. Enchanté."

Once again, Alex took her mother's hand. They placed the same lips that had touched hers the night before on the back of Catherine's limp wrist. Was the sudden uncomfortableness inside of her jealousy? She had felt hints of it when Catherine paid more attention to whoever was on the phone than she did to her, but this was something different. It was heightened.

Like awkward anger mixed with a dash of melancholy.

The feeling went away instantly when Alex turned to embrace her. An electric hug that shocked them apart immediately. Partly because of the intensity behind it and partly because neither wanted to show too much affection in front of the others.

What Seneca really wanted for her birthday was some more alone time with Alex. Even if it meant another clandestine meeting in the middle of the night.

"Seneca, happy birthday!"

"Thank you so much, Alex. Come in the living room and meet the Coyvilles. The couple from Jude Lake I was telling you about."

Before long, dinner was being served. Marie gathered their friends at the dining room table, which was adorned with a handcrafted centrepiece made out of orange tree branches and Seneca's favourite flowers.

"Mama C, this is beautiful! Thank you so much. It's breathtaking."

"Don't look at me," said Catherine, shifting her eyes in Alex's direction.

Seneca turned to Alex. "You made this?"

They held up both hands in surrender. "Guilty as charged."

"How did you know which flowers were my favourite?"

"Catherine said it was okay to cut some fresh from the garden. I simply picked the ones that reminded me of you."

"Well, they're perfect." *You're perfect.* "Thank you."

"My pleasure."

Everyone took their places at the table. Seneca next to Alex. Exactly where she wanted to be.

The table was brimming with chicken, ribs, and every vegetable grown under the sun. There were potatoes cooked four different ways. By the end of the meal, Seneca wasn't sure she had tasted everything.

Though she was certain she couldn't take another bite.

Cake was put on the backburner until they had time to digest dinner. In the meantime, they gathered back in the living room to open presents. She unwrapped gift after gift, each one more thoughtful than the one before it.

The Coyvilles gave her a new deck of cards.

"Now, you can stop using the joker as the ace of spades," said Ernest.

Seneca laughed. "That's so considerate. Thank you, Ernest."

"It was Helen's idea," he replied, and they all laughed.

"Well thank you both." She inhaled deeply. "Mmmmmm, there's nothing like the smell of a fresh deck."

JD gave her five new books. She had read all but one.

Her mothers presented her with a gold necklace. The chain toted one half of a charm. It was the right side of a heart that had been split down the middle.

"Where's the other half?" she asked.

Catherine and Marie exchanged a knowing glance between them.

"We're not *exactly* sure, Seneca. But we have faith that someday you'll discover it."

Typical Marie response.

After all of the gifts were unwrapped, Alex stood up from the couch.

"I'll be performing my gift."

Seneca's heart skipped a beat. Alex crossed the room, grabbed Marie's guitar and strummed a few notes to confirm it was in tune.

"I wrote a song for you, Seneca. It was inspired by the brief but insightful conversations we've had since we met."

"Just yesterday."

"Yes. One day ago. Which leads perfectly into this tune. It's called, 'One Day'."

The guitar started to sing. A true musician at the helm. Then Alex's voice filled the room.

Adulthood knocked on my door today
Although no words were spoken
I suddenly feel like a kid again
So, I purposely failed to open

One single day was all it took
One special person, one special look
One single day was all it took
One day, one look, I'm hooked

Was this actually happening? Seneca was on cloud nine. She tried to focus on the words Alex was singing, but it was the emotion behind their performance that was taking her breath away. Tears filled her eyes. Joyful tears. This was by far her best birthday ever. Not in a million years could she have dreamed up a better day.

Yeah, one single day
Just look, I'm shook
One day, one look
I'm hooked

Alex's voice was spellbinding. She already knew that from their time together in the orange grove. If she didn't know how they felt before, it was clear now. Alex was just as smitten as she was. Their song was proof of that.

Tears spilled down her face by the time Alex played the final note.

"That was beyond beautiful. For once, for real, I'm speechless."

Alex passed the guitar to Marie without looking away from Seneca. It felt like they were the only two in the room until Catherine interrupted.

"I'm ready to sing a few tunes if you want to put that guitar to good use, Marie."

"Oh, please do!" said Ernest. "I wouldn't mind a couple of fast songs. See if Helen can still keep up with me on the dance floor."

"You'll be begging for a rest before I'm warmed up," Helen retorted.

"Grab the bongos, Sen," said Catherine. "Let's take the Coyvilles on a little trip back in time."

For over an hour they danced and sang. They had only planned to perform one song but it turned into an all-out jam session. Everyone took turns playing different instruments.

They all sang.

When they had worked off their dinner and worked up an appetite, Seneca blew out sixteen candles. They devoured an entire cake in one sitting.

"I suppose we should hit the road," said Ernest, yawning as he took his last bite. "Tomorrow is a big day and Seneca needs her sleep."

"Seneca, eh?" said Helen. "Looks like she's not the only one who could use a little shuteye."

They saw them out and reconvened in the living room. Seneca was anxious to get Alex alone again. Out of the corner of her eye, she caught Marie setting up the picture boards. Time for the story of Seneca's miracle conception and birth.

It would be a good twenty minutes before the party was over.

Everyone in the room had heard it before, except Alex.

This would be the last time the story was told if she didn't survive the Light Ceremony. The story was the reason she was a Light Seeker. If Alex wanted to learn more about her, it was a great place to start.

Catherine and Marie always told the story together. Word for word. Details never changed.

Everyone around Seneca believed in her destiny. There was no reason to question it.

Or was there?

As her moms recalled precious moments from sixteen years ago, she recalled tense moments from the night before.

What had they been arguing about? Bits and pieces of their conversation came flooding back. Catherine, saying it was too late to back out. Marie, calling her a pawn.

Overcome by a wave of nausea, she excused herself to use the washroom.

"We'll pause the story until you get back, sweetie," suggested Catherine.

"Keep going. I'll be quick."

She wet her hands under the tap and splashed her face. The cold water shocked her system. So be it. Life was shocking her system.

Until yesterday, her life's path had been straightforward. Her goal was to become a Light Seeker. Every move she made and every thought she had led back to that.

But in twenty-four hours, her clear-cut path was suddenly filled with twists and turns.

The argument was weighing heavy on her mind and Alex's presence was bringing up new emotions. It was as though her reason for existing had shifted after meeting them. No longer was she just a Light Seeker who was there to satisfy the needs of others until she carried out her purpose. Now she was an individual with her own thoughts and feelings.

Maybe someday, her own goals.

No one ever talked about what *she* would do when they made it to Light City. It was as though arriving there was the ultimate achievement. Nothing came after.

Or had she refused to allow herself to think about what came afterwards before she made it through the Light Ceremony?

Seneca didn't know.

One thing she *did* know. If she didn't get back to the party soon, someone would come looking for her.

All eyes shifted in her direction when she returned to the living room.

"I'm back." She flashed them a reassuring smile. "Have I been born?"

"Not yet," said Catherine. "Marie just finished telling the story of how we met and fell in love."

"Look at how young we were here."

Marie pointed to one of the picture boards. She singled out a photograph of her and Catherine, sitting on a pile of wood, laughing away. Barely in their 20's and both extremely attractive. Although Catherine had always cared more about her appearance than Marie. Her long, blonde locks were always perfectly styled. Her make-up, on point.

No enhancements were needed when it came to Marie. She was a natural beauty. Ma still had the same long, dark hair she'd had in her younger years. Smooth as silk. Always parted down the middle. Sometimes in braids when she was building something, but typically left to hang freely.

"This picture was taken the day we started to build this house," said Marie.

"Later that day, our lives would change forever," added Catherine.

JD's eyes glazed over. His lack of interest was apparent. Who could blame him? He had heard the story many times before.

Alex was heavily invested.

Catherine had already explained how they met on a hot summer day when Marie was building a new ocean-view deck for the Ellis family. She brought Marie a glass of water to help her cool down and their relationship heated up from there.

It was love at first sight.

For the next several weeks they spent all their waking hours together. Marie finished the deck and completed a few other projects around the Ellis home. Catherine would set up a chair and lounge around in glamorous swimsuits, rambling on and on while Marie hammered away.

This continued until Mr. Ellis took notice and told Marie her services were no longer required.

Catherine begged her father to keep Marie on staff. After all, they were looking to hire a full-time handy person. But he refused and forbade his daughter from seeing Marie again.

No one told Catherine what to do.

Later that day, she stashed some valuables under her massive skirt and threw on her famous red crop top. The top was enough to distract all eyes, as she strutted through the main gates and into The Darkness, without so much as a glance behind her.

The rest of the party was a bit of a blur. Seneca was focused on figuring out a way to get some alone time with Alex. That was all she needed. Then she would be able to drift off. Enjoy one final sleep in their log cabin before moving to Light City.

Or would it be one final sleep before the 'big sleep'?

Focus.

Seneca refused to let her thoughts become fears. Her thoughts were her allies. Any negativity was stopped in its tracks. Instead, she formulated a plan to return to the orange grove.

"I can't thank you enough for this amazing birthday party. All of you. This has definitely been the best one yet."

"You're welcome, sweetie. We love you so much," said Catherine.

"I love you too," replied Seneca. "Well, guess it's time to get some sleep."

They walked JD and Alex to the door, sending them off with an abundance of hugs and kisses. Before their final farewell, Seneca leaned in to say goodnight to Alex.

"Meet me under the orange tree," she whispered.

The RSVP in Alex's eyes said it all.

Attending.

CHAPTER 18

A RETURN TO THE ORANGE GROVE

It was close to midnight. Yet the sky resembled dusk. The full Buck Moon was less than a week away. Must be why. Whatever the reason, Seneca could see Alex sitting under the orange tree clearly from thirty feet away.

"We only have a few minutes left to celebrate your birthday."

Seneca wrapped her ankle-length nightgown around her thighs. She bunched the extra material at the small of her back so she could sit comfortably.

They leaned on each other instead of the tree.

It was several minutes before either spoke. A great deal had already been said that night. Alex would likely have questions about her miracle conception and birth. It was certainly a lot for the average person to take in.

Not that Alex was even close to average.

"Thank you for the song. It was the best gift anyone has ever given me. Even though I couldn't unwrap it, and I love to unwrap presents."

"Okay, I see you. How about this? On your next birthday, I'll get you something you can unwrap."

"Promise?"

"Cross my heart."

That was an entire year from now. Did that mean they wanted to be a part of her life long after the Light Ceremony?

It was all happening so fast. If only she could stop time.

Her wristwatch read 11:54 p.m.

Sleep was more important tonight than any other night of her life. Somehow that didn't matter. In the moment, quality alone time with Alex seemed more important.

"Quite the story of how you were conceived. It sounds like a Christian bible tale. Do you believe it?"

Do I believe it? The topic didn't catch her off guard, but Alex's question certainly did. Of course she believed it.

She had lived it.

It was her story.

"I'm not really sure what you mean. I'm here on this earth. The product of two women. Born from the womb of one and identical to the other. Sure, it sounds like a fairytale but it's my life."

"Please don't be offended. It wasn't my intent to call your life into question."

"I know. It's a lot to take in." Seneca stirred the dirt at her feet with her bare toes.

"An angel appearing before your moms. Telling them a child would be born unto them. A baby girl who would help bring the world out of the darkness and into the light? Yeah, it's a lot."

"You don't have to believe it. Just respect that it's what I believe."

Silence fell between them. Less comfortable than some of their past shared quiet time. Why was she so defensive? Maybe because Alex was way off base. Or was it because she herself was starting to doubt the validity of her origin story?

"I have the utmost respect for you, Seneca. I was worried about you. That's all. You took off to the washroom halfway through the story. When you returned you still looked like Marie, but your complexion was as white as Catherine's."

"*Ah ha*, you see! I'm definitely a mix of those two women."

The winds picked up. An air of lightheartedness fell over them. Alex pulled her close. Rested one arm over her shoulder. With their free hand, they pointed to a scar on Seneca's leg.

"How did you get that?"

Seneca ran her fingertips across the old wound. It ran vertical along the back of her right calf and measured about an inch in length. She hadn't thought about it in years.

"This happened shortly after your cousin moved in next door."

"JD did this to you when you were just a kid?"

"No, no!" she snorted. "It happened at his house though. One minute I was playing with the chickens in the yard and the next thing I knew, I was laying in my bed with ten stitches in the back of my leg."

"What happened?"

"You know, I'm still not entirely sure to this day. My moms told me I tripped and hit my head. Knocked myself unconscious. But when I woke up my head felt fine. My leg on the other hand. Ouch!"

"May I touch it?"

"Sure."

Alex ran their thumb over the top of her scar. Back and forth. Smooth strokes. Something about their touch made Seneca feel relaxed and excited simultaneously. If only she could stay in this moment forever.

Tomorrow, time was not her own.

Sunrise to sunset, the day of the Light Ceremony was regimented in rigid ceremonial tradition. From what she ate and drank, to who she saw throughout the course of the day and who was allowed in the Waiting Room before the ceremony. Only immediate family members were permitted to say their goodbyes in the room inside the Crow Line.

In Seneca's case, that was Catherine and Marie.

"How are you feeling about the Light Ceremony tomorrow?" asked Alex.

Good question.

Excited. Nervous. Anxious. Afraid?

The fear didn't stem from the ceremony itself. She was confident she could pass all Seven Steps. Up until yesterday, Seneca was mostly afraid of disappointing her moms. Now, she had the added fear of missing out on a relationship with Alex. Who she was...falling in love with? No, it was too soon for that.

Wasn't it?

Catherine and Marie had fallen in love at first sight. It was definitely something that happened to people.

She kept her answer simple. "I guess I'm feeling mostly excited."

Alex peered down at their watch. "Let me rephrase that. How are you feeling about the Light Ceremony later today? It's midnight."

"Excellent. If I can't have you in the Waiting Room with my loved ones before the ceremony, at least I can spend a bit of time with you on what could be my final day."

"Don't say that! You're going to smash those steps. I'll be singing for you and the family at Lupia's days from now. Listening to your moms recall tales of your bravery."

"Speaking of my moms, I hope they don't discover I'm gone. I waited for over an hour after they turned out the lights. But those women seem to have a strange sixth sense when it comes to my whereabouts."

"Oh yeah?"

"*Ohhh* yeah! A few years ago, I wandered deeper into the woods than I normally do and got turned around. Night moved in before I could find the path. I decided to wait it out until morning, knowing if I started out on foot at night there was a chance I'd wander farther from home. Plus, wild animals and stuff."

"That must have been so scary."

"Not really. I train to survive. Anyway, I climbed a tall tree nearby to get a good lay of the land and that's when I heard footsteps. Three figures appeared under the tree. I heard JD's voice say something like, 'she has to be here'. Somehow, they had managed to locate me."

"Maybe the scar on your leg is from where they inserted the tracker."

"Not funny!" she grinned. "Although I wouldn't put it past them. Considering the amount of rules I have to follow as a Light Seeker, they do give me plenty of freedom to roam."

"I can't imagine the life you've led. It's fascinating, really."

Seneca took hold of Alex's hand. "The *lives* I've led. It's as though there are two. One life I live for others. The other life I dream of living for myself. I guess most people could say that. It's just that mine comes with a timeline. Sixteen years of living for others and if I've done everything right, then I can have the life I dream of. My moms too."

"An extreme amount of pressure to place on one person."

"I can handle it. It's my destiny."

"Well, don't let me keep you. Your destiny awaits! I want you to get plenty of sleep, selfishly, so that tomorrow night you'll still be awake enough to celebrate with me on the other side."

"That sounds like something from the life I dream of."

Alex leaned in. Their lips encased her own. It was a kiss that took her breath away. A kiss that made her feel alive. A kiss that lingered long after they had said goodnight and she was back in her bed.

Safely tucked beneath the covers.

Laying in stillness in their log cabin, she thought back to when she was a girl who dreamed of finding love in Light City. In order to do that, she had to be a successful Light Seeker. Must complete all Seven Steps Into The Light. That was the only way to find love.

Or so she thought.

As she drifted off in The Darkness, Seneca came to an important realization. She didn't need to step into the light to find love.

There was love in the dark.

CHAPTER 19

THE LIGHT CEREMONY BEGINS

Saturday, July 9th, 2022

President Barbara Crow glanced at the clock in the study. In less than ten minutes she had to leave for the Light Ceremony. Where was her father? He should be here by now. Sure, Walter was a busy man and his time was precious. Well, she was a busy woman and her time was also precious. *She* was precious. Soon, he would recognize that.

Perhaps he would even call her his 'little Barbie' again.

General Walter Crow was a true hero. King of Barsicon, even though he scoffed at the title. Kings were weak, he'd told her growing up. Generals took care of business and that is what her father did. Took care of business.

Whatever that business may be.

Barsicon was *her* business.

Her baby brother Obadiah was too slow of mind to aid Walter in the way he required. A childhood tragedy at the boathouse changed him forever. Consequently, Barbara was raised to be her father's protégé.

For two decades, she had executed his agenda, as President. Finally, she was unfolding an idea that was all her own; a plan to better Barsicon *and* heal her relationship with Walter.

Her daddy.

If only she had paid more attention that fateful morning by the ocean.

Life would be so different.

To this day, she had nightmares about it. Nightmares that seemed so real she could feel her toes in the sand while she slept. See her brother's body being pulled from the water. Hear the shouts from her father. Yelling for her to get help.

It was a day that would haunt her forever.

The day four-year-old Obadiah's mind stopped growing at the same quick pace as his body and never caught up.

Barbara heard footsteps outside the study. She quickly wiped away a single tear that had escaped and spilled down her cheek. The General would not be pleased to see her display such weakness.

Not once had she seen her father cry, and on the rare occasion her mother shed a tear, he was quick to tell her to stop. Walter would point to their vast kingdom and gently remind his wife that she had nothing to cry about.

"My apologies, Barbara," said Walter brusquely. "I was waiting for your mother and Obadiah but they're running behind. They'll meet us in the limousine in five."

"That's fine. There's something I need to discuss with you anyway."

"Does it have to do with this crime and punishment plan you refuse to tell me about? Frankly, I'm a bit worried."

"Don't be worried. Please trust me. I've put my heart and soul into this project. I know you'll approve once you see it laid out."

Walter raised one red eyebrow. "Why the secrecy?"

"Patience. When you see the plan, it will all make sense."

"Good because right now it makes no sense. You are the only person working on this project. How do you expect to implement an entirely new plan without a single soul besides you having knowledge of it?"

"Have I not promised to show you the plan before it becomes public? That's actually what I wanted to talk to you about. The night before the news conference, I would like for the entire family to have dinner together at the castle. In the formal dining hall."

"Will I get details then?"

"Yes. Also, I'd like to make a special request that you stop by the study to escort me to dinner. Alone. Have mother and Obadiah meet us there."

"My daughter, you're acting strange. I don't like it."

"You don't like it because you don't know what it's all about. But soon you will. Once you do, you won't just like it. You'll love it. You'll love me...," said Barbara.

Again.

"Let's go," said Walter. "We're going to be late for the ceremony."

Barbara draped her white ceremonial cloak over her shoulders and followed Walter out the door to the limo.

By the time they arrived at the main gates, the crowd was already anxious to get the ceremony underway. The weekly spectacle was the only activity all Barsiconians enjoyed together. Whether you lived in Light City or The Darkness, you were at the main gates on Saturday night for the action.

Even a few of the Northern Warriors on duty stopped and watched in amusement during their patrols.

Barbara noticed Walter join Obadiah and Tilly in their private viewing box. How was it possible that her mother looked younger than she did? Yes, she had given birth to Barbara as a teenager. Still, you would think the extra fifteen years would show.

They didn't.

Not in the slightest.

The pressures of ruling Barsicon were having visible effects on Barbara. Work, work, work. It was all she did. Almost every waking hour.

Work.

A word her mother knew nothing about. Tilly's posh lifestyle was stress-free. Apart from doting on Obadiah, she honestly had no idea how her mother spent her days.

The Crow family's viewing box was built on the fourth step. Front row seats for the fight. Plus, a great view of the three steps below and above.

Light Seekers' family members and a few friends were allowed to follow them up each step and watch from the sidelines. Residents of The Darkness craned their necks to watch from the ground below, while citizens of Light City took their choice of seats on one of the Seven Steps.

Tonight, thousands gathered to witness history.

The youngest to ever seek the light stood bare footed on the first step.

Long hair hung over her right shoulder. The left side was cut short to her head. No question, she was ready to recite the Crow Code. Barbara could see the girl was focused. For someone so young, she was remarkably composed.

Hopefully, she wouldn't get herself killed before the fifth step. After that, there was little room for error. Assuming she could successfully slaughter that obnoxious warrior Hale on the fourth step. They used to call him Speedy because he was the fastest in the north. These days, he was sluggish at best.

The girl should have no problem with tonight's giant.

Or his giant ego.

"The mind is a powerful thing. On the third step, we will challenge your knowledge. Seven questions. Each one harder than its predecessor. Light Seeker, are you prepared to prove your mental superiority?"

"I am, Madam President."

"We shall proceed."

Just as she suspected, the young Light Seeker had no problems reciting the Crow Code. Seneca had also practically flown through the obstacle course. Barbara would have to check, but she was quite certain the girl completed it in record time. Now she was whizzing through the Mind Challenge.

The young Light Seeker answered every question without hesitation.

"In 2004, approximately 2,000 Ferox Caninovours in the Northern Forest were killed during what?"

"Den Demolishing Day."

"Correct. What is the middle name of the famous composer, Hektor Eason?"

"Cletus."

Back and forth they went until all seven questions were asked and answered correctly.

Then she made her way to the fourth step.

While the girl took her place in the fighting circle, Barbara passed by the Crow's viewing box.

Obadiah threw popcorn at his mouth. A couple of pieces actually made it in. Walter chatted nearby with some of his men. Tilly smiled for the people. Yet somehow still managed to look sad.

Why was her mother always so troubled?

Queen Tilly's life hadn't been that hard. Sure, she had lost her family at a young age. But Walter had saved her. Cared for her.

She should consider herself lucky. Not only was she drop dead gorgeous, she was powerful.

Most importantly, she was loved by Walter.

Her father's affection towards her mother was the real source of her jealousy. That and her mother's shiny black hair.

It was simply stunning.

Barbara loved her father. More than anything. But she could have done without his twisted red locks.

CHAPTER 20

HOLD MY HAND, MATILDA

Thursday, April 27th, 1972

Walter Crow ran down the hallway in Jordhar Castle and threw open the bedroom door. The King had reached the climax of his bedtime story. He held up a finger, not wanting to be disturbed at the height of his tale.

"Tilly had to fight off four giants and three fire-breathing dragons. That wasn't all..."

"I'm sorry to interrupt, my King," Walter gasped. "This can't wait."

Whatever his trusted advisor was about to say was not something Matilda should hear. He could already tell Walter's hasty appearance had frightened her.

King Quinton kissed his daughter on the forehead. "Stay here, Tilly. I'll be right back."

"Okay, daddy. Hurry."

He closed the door gently behind him. The King peered down the empty hallway. Where were his guards? Two soldiers were supposed to be stationed between the twins' room and the royal bedchamber at all times.

"Sir, we have to get you out of here. Grab the girl and run!"

"Whoa, slow down," said King Quinton. "What are you talking about?"

"It's terrible. I'm sorry to be the one to tell you this, but it's Queen Raya. She's dead."

"Dead? Walter, you're speaking nonsense. Where are Raya and Millie?"

"I'll explain as soon as we get to a safe place. We must leave right away."

"I'm not leaving here without my family," he roared and started down the hallway.

"King Quinton! Please, stop. You don't want to go in there."

"Go get Tilly and take her to the study. Have her show you how to open the secret room. Stay there until I tell you it's safe to come out. Do you understand?"

"Yes, your majesty. As you wish," Walter bowed.

King Quinton sprinted down the hallway. Raya was dead? That was impossible. They had just made love. Moments ago, they were telling bedtime stories to their precious daughters. Was Mildred with her mother?

Had the soldiers run in to help them?

He pushed through the unguarded door and breathed a sigh of relief when he saw his two men relaxed and smiling. Relief turned to shock, as he stepped further into the room and took in the entire scene.

Gasp!

The two soldiers moved in and grabbed him by both arms. His own men, there to protect him from harm, were now dragging him towards the most horrific display he had ever laid eyes on.

Lying lifeless on the floor was his beautiful wife.

Desperately, he fought to come to grips with reality. The love of his life had been terrified when she died. Her frozen, frightened expression said it all.

It broke his heart in two.

A vainglorious General Homer Thomson stood over Queen Raya's body.

"Your wife didn't like me barging in on her. As you can see, I didn't care for her attitude," he smirked.

King Quinton struggled to break free from the guards. "I will kill you with my bare hands, you son of a bitch!"

"You'll have to. Unless you're cleverly hiding something in that nightshirt, my guess is you're not armed."

"What do you want? I don't understand!"

"Understand this," he said, seizing King Quinton by his beard. "I am the kind of man who takes what he wants, and I want Barsicon."

General Thomson yanked him onto the balcony. Down below, soldiers lined the streets, setting fires and beating innocent people who dared to step outside their homes to see what the fuss was about. Officers from the Barsicon Police Force raced to help, armed with flashlights and batons, only to be gunned down in cold blood.

The military leader forced the King to watch the horrendous scene play out for several minutes before he ordered the two soldiers to stand down.

"Let him go. I'll deal with him from here."

The soldiers released King Quinton's arms and he dropped to the ground, defeated. He took one last look around his room in Jordhar Castle. How had his life shattered into a million pieces in a matter of minutes?

He looked at the bed he shared with his beautiful wife, who lay completely still on the other side.

Not everything was still.

A pillow moved up and down. The movement was slight. But it was enough to tear the King's heart open one more time.

Mildred.

She was still alive and in obvious danger.

Raya had been smart enough to draw the curtain on one side of the bed, shielding their daughter from witnessing her death. But from the balcony where he stood, should his daughter peek out from under the blanket, she would have a clear view of his demise.

"Any last words?"

King Quinton pushed himself to his feet and moved closer to the bed to ensure his daughter could hear him.

"Yes, I do have something to say." He paused to choose his next words wisely.

"Get on with it!" Homer shouted impatiently.

"I love you with all my heart." A message for Mildred. "Meet me in the secret room for one final bedtime story."

Had Walter and Matilda made it there safely?

He turned away from the bed and faced off with General Thomson.

His chances of surviving were slim, but he wouldn't go down without a fight.

King Quinton took one step forward before a bullet from the General's gun blew him back onto the bed. The King landed directly on top of two small legs that trembled under red satin sheets.

Mildred remained as motionless as her father for several minutes. When all was quiet, she slid her legs out from under him and threw off the covers.

Go to the study.

Her father wouldn't be there for one final bedtime story, but maybe someone else would be. Someone who could help her.

Matilda!

Mildred decided to stop by their shared bedroom on the way. In case her sister was still there.

The large wooden door creaked as it opened. Mildred peered into the empty corridor. From the hallway, she could hear the street riots below. The princess slipped into her bedroom.

"Tilly are you here?" she whispered. "Come out if you're hiding. We have to get to the secret room right away!"

Frantic, she searched under the beds and inside the closet for her sister. Twin instincts told her Matilda was still alive and that she had to find her.

Their parents were dead.

All they had left was each other.

But how would she get to the secret room? Then it hit her!

Thoughts of her sister gave Mildred the surge of bravery she needed. Channelling her twin, she threw open the laundry chute hatch. Matilda was always getting in trouble for sliding down it and Mildred had always been too scared to try.

She saw no other choice.

The chute led to the laundry room, which was next to the study. If soldiers were guarding the hallway downstairs, the laundry chute would be her best chance to get to the secret room without being seen.

Mildred jumped through the hole in the wall and slid down one floor. She landed softly on top of a pile of dirty linens.

Her twin had been right.

It was fun.

She instantly regretted not trying it sooner.

Inside the secret room, Matilda sat in the King's wingback armchair. Her legs weren't long enough to reach the matching royal blue ottoman in front. She used to sit on the footstool with her sister and listen to their father read from books that lined three of the four walls.

The fourth wall was the magic wall.

It was a showstopper in the study. A massive, limestone fireplace. On the mantle was a candlestick that when pushed back twice, and pulled forward once, would trigger the floor in front of the fireplace to spin. Within three seconds of handling the candlestick, whoever was standing in front of the fireplace was in the secret room.

Only members of the royal Jordhar family knew about it.

Now, so did Walter Crow.

He knelt down next to Matilda. Met the sobbing princess at eye level. Grabbed hold of her small hand.

"There, there. It's okay. I know you're scared. Don't worry. Your dad will be here to get us soon."

"What if he doesn't come back? What if the giants are attacking us for real?"

"Tilly," Walter started.

"My name is Matilda," she rebutted.

"I'm sorry. Matilda." He softened his voice. "If your parents don't come back, I promise to take care of you until the day you are able to take care of yourself. I give you my word."

"Where is my sister? We have to find Mildred!"

"I'm going to find her right now. You have to stay here. Do not leave the study. Under any circumstances. Okay?"

"Okay." She wiped tears onto the sleeve of her nightgown. "Be careful."

"I'll check in soon. With any luck, I'll have Mildred with me."

Walter placed a hand on the ottoman and pushed himself to his feet. Matilda jumped up. Her bare feet sunk into the cushioned armchair. She wrapped her arms around Walter's neck.

"I just want to see my family."

"I know, Matilda. I'm going to do everything within my power to find them and bring them back to you."

The princess sat back in the chair and mumbled something.

"Pardon me?"

"Tilly." She said it clearly the second time. "You can call me Tilly."

A single wall separated the twins from each other. There was no way for them to know it. Even if they did, there was no way for them to bust through it.

Mildred stood with her ear pressed to the laundry room door. She listened for sounds from the hallway. The study was right around the corner. Before she made her move, she had to make sure the coast was clear.

Silence.

Thankfully, she could no longer hear screams or gunfire from the streets. She turned the knob slowly, opened the door an inch and waited.

Still, silence.

Twin instincts told her Matilda was close by. Her sister had made it to the secret room, she just knew it! Mildred was determined to join her there.

Satisfied the path was clear, she opened the door another inch before she heard footsteps and retreated under a sheet. Through a crack in the doorway she saw two sets of feet. Two soldiers marched past the laundry room and stopped in front of the study.

A third pair of feet appeared.

"Sir, we have a big problem."

"Huge. Giants from the Northern Forest are descending on Barsicon. They're slaughtering our men by the masses."

The soldiers were talking to Walter Crow.

"Where's Homer?"

"He's upstairs on the balcony and he's asking to see you," the first soldier replied. "What do you want us to do, sir?"

"Tell me who you answer to. Is it me, or do you answer to General Thomson?"

In unison. "We answer to you, sir."

"Good. Listen up, I have a mission for you. One of the twin girls is safe with me. The other one is still missing. Mildred. I need you to find her immediately."

Mildred breathed a huge sigh of relief. Her prayers had been answered. Matilda was safe next door. Walter was protecting her sister and he would protect her too. For the first time since her parents' death, she felt a glimmer of hope.

There was no need to make them search for her. Mildred peeled herself from beneath the sheet on the laundry room floor. Her legs nearly gave out as she stood. She reached for the knob, ready to swing the door open to safety---

"What should we do with the girl when we find her?"

"Get rid of her," commanded Walter. "When I'm ruler of Barsicon, I'll only need one Queen."

CHAPTER 21

THE LIGHT CEREMONY ENDS

Saturday, July 9th, 2022

Adrenaline coursed through her body.

The first three steps were fun. Especially the obstacle course. The alligators did their best to throw her off. The creatures snapped at her while she cleared the course above them, but she refused to be their dinner.

Next step: Fight A Warrior.

The kill would have to be quick. Seneca needed to save energy for her baptism. After that, she would plead her case. But now wasn't the time to get ahead of herself.

The largest man she had ever seen in real life had just ascended onto the fourth step.

Like all Northern Warriors, his bald head was covered in tattoos. Seneca counted eleven golden rings climbing up his lengthy beard. An enormous grin was smeared across his face and he had a cocky air about him. As though he had already won the fight.

Perfect.

One thing she counted on was being underestimated and it was clear this warrior was not taking her seriously.

The giant's grin turned into a chuckle as she stepped closer. His chuckle morphed into an all-out belly laugh when she stood tall and stared him dead in the eye.

"Well, look what we have here!" he howled. "A little girl who thinks she can take on a real warrior. Are you prepared to die?"

Seneca gave the warrior the silent treatment.

"Nothing to say? Go ahead, speak! These are gonna be your final words, so make 'em count."

Seneca remained voiceless.

In a minute, she would shut him up for good.

President Crow took her place at the podium. "To enter Light City, a Light Seeker must fight their way in. This battle ends when a life ends. May the God of Light have mercy on your soul. Fight!"

The crowd let out a deafening roar. Seneca desperately wanted to give her family a reassuring smile and let them know they had no reason to fear. Of course, she couldn't. Not with a Northern Warrior circling.

Cheers and taunts rang loud.

Alex's voice stood out among the rest. "Come on, Seneca. You've got this!"

Their shouts of encouragement pushed Seneca into action.

The Northern Warrior was much larger than her. Much larger and much slower. With his arms outstretched, the giant waved his hands up and down to get the crowd excited. It worked.

The roars intensified.

Just the cue she needed.

While the warrior focused on entertaining the crowd, Seneca moved in.

Three quick strides and she was in front of the giant. She clutched the bottom of his ringed beard and used it to propel herself over his shoulder. The warrior threw his hands behind his head to try and catch her, but he was too slow.

Seneca slid down her opponent's rear, kicking him in the back of the knee on her way to the ground. The massive man buckled. She used the back of his calf to springboard her way up to his shoulders.

The warrior spun around in circles, trying to toss her from his back. Seneca held steady and placed him in a rear naked choke. They struggled; the warrior to breathe and Seneca to hang on.

Should she keep him in this chokehold?

Seneca wasn't sure if she could hold on long enough to render the warrior unconscious. It was clear what had to be done and it had to be done quickly.

An image of Cooper popped into her mind as she snapped the warrior's neck. From beginning to end, the fight lasted thirty seconds.

If only her baptism would pass that quickly.

The water was colder than she expected. Seneca didn't bother to count off the seconds or minutes in her mind. It would only worry her. A lifetime of training in the pond told her she was well beyond the two-minute mark.

Had kissing Alex doomed her?

They had kissed so many times.

Did she dare open her eyes? The tank was transparent. Maybe she would be able to spot her loved ones. No. If she opened her eyes to search for them it might cause her to panic.

Dear God of Light, when is this going to be over?

A picture of Catherine's chalkboard appeared in her mind. It was a reminder that she had held her breath for almost eight minutes on her final training day. If she had to stay under for that length of time again, there was a chance---

An alarm went off.

It was the sound she was waiting for.

The siren was muffled until the lid of the tank opened and she emerged from the water. Then it became ear piercing. Seneca pressed her wet palms against the sides of her head to dull the sweetest sound she had ever heard.

Her baptism was complete!

Now all she had to do was deliver 300 carefully crafted words on the sixth step and wait for the white smoke to engulf her in the glass box on the seventh.

Light City was so close she could taste it.

It tasted like freedom.

•———•

"For these reasons, I humbly ask that you grant permission to the Ellis-Brant family to enter Light City. It is with great admiration that I make this request, Madam President. Admiration and respect for you, the Crow family, Light City and all of Barsicon. Thank you."

Seneca bowed and waited for her instructions.

"Thank you, Light Seeker. I will now confer with the God of Light while you make your way to the glass box where you will await Final Judgement."

Her destiny was within sight.

Only one more step.

From the seventh step, she could see into Light City. The view was incredible. It exceeded the magical pictures she had conjured up in her mind over the years.

Crow Coliseum was massive and magnificent!

It had so much green space for a city, and the buildings. Oh, the buildings! They were a sight of beauty. Many were held up by sturdy columns. Each property had its own extravagant features. There were fountains everywhere and balconies made of marble.

In the middle of it all, superior to the rest, was Crow Castle.

A grand fortress.

The towering stone palace was surrounded by armed members of the BPF and unarmed Northern Warriors. The giants needed no weapons. Their presence alone was terrifying. A wooden drawbridge adorned the front of the castle. The only thing it lacked was a moat.

Indeed, Light City was truly sublime.

All of it nestled along the West Ocean. A body of water so vast, she couldn't see where it ended.

So this was it.

For the first time since the Light Ceremony began, Seneca scanned the masses.

No surprise, she spotted Alex first.

JD stood next to his cousin. He smiled and pumped his fist with excitement. No doubt he was so proud of her for taking down that huge Northern Warrior. He had trained her well.

Why did her mothers appear so distraught?

All they had ever wanted was to move to Light City and it was about to happen. She was about to make it happen for all of them.

Her baptism clocked in at 2:47. Below average. The obstacle course had been a breeze and President Crow seemed pleased with her case for getting into Light City.

All she had left to do was step into the glass box and step out into the light.

A simple formality.

Clouds appeared overhead. If the sky opened up and a beam of light shone down on them, she would be a successful Light Seeker.

President Crow closed the door to the glass box and locked it. Seneca blew a kiss to her loved ones.

Little did she know, she was blowing them a kiss goodbye.

A hissing sound at her feet. She lowered her head and watched the gray smoke start to fill the glass box.

It always starts out gray. It's fine.

By the time it reached knee height, it would change to black or white. Those were the only options.

Please, please clear!

The gray smoke continued to rise.

It wasn't clearing.

Seneca did her best to stay calm. Her moms clung to each other on the sidelines. Alex had placed an arm around JD, who was no longer fist-pumping the air. He was biting his nails instead. Everyone had a look of death about them. Even Marie's bronze complexion had paled to white.

What was *not* white was the smoke that encircled her waist.

It was a dark gray and growing darker by the second.

She had been to enough Light Ceremonies to know the smoke never turned white once it reached waist height.

It should be clearing!

This couldn't be happening. Was she dreaming? The clouds overhead were still closed tight. There would be no beam of light shining through them tonight.

Seneca looked at President Crow's expressionless face. Or *was* it expressionless? Had the leader of Barsicon just given her a small, knowing smile?

Cough, cough.

Smoke entered her lungs. Maybe she could hold her breath long enough to escape? Not likely. Not without taking a few deep breaths first.

Her poor Mama C and Ma Marie were out there, probably panicked and crying. Or so she guessed. There was no way to know for sure. She couldn't see them anymore. The entire glass box was one big plume of black smoke.

Certain death was near.

Tears streamed down her face. No sense holding them back now. Seneca took a small breath through her nose. She inhaled the fumes and immediately started coughing. The locked door wouldn't budge. She tried it twice. Even if she did get out, rules were rules. Time to admit defeat.

It was over.

Even though her eyes were closed, and no one could see her cry, she wiped the tears from her face. For some reason it gave her strength in a hopeless situation.

Why prolong the inevitable?

Attempting to stay alive at this point was torture.

Deprived of oxygen, Seneca slipped into unconsciousness. Her limp body dropped to the floor of the glass box at the exact same time the floor gave way.

PART 2

CHAPTER 22

A TIME FOR TEARS

Wednesday, September 12th, 2001

There was only one other person in the park. A man. He was sitting on a bench at the opposite end of the grounds. Head in his hands. Was he crying? Yes, he was. Good. It gave her permission to do the same.

Barbara sobbed.

She was soaking wet. Covered in tears and sweat. She must have run two miles to this park from Crow Castle following another argument with Walter. Her father. Who insisted she call him Walter.

Or General Crow.

His actual preference.

Today's argument was far worse than any of their past disputes. Walter was fuming over her latest attempt to win back his love.

Perhaps she should go live on one of the ghost islands. Alone. What was the point of trying to win back his love? She lost his affection when she was seven. When she was left in charge of her brother at the boathouse.

The day Obadiah drowned and came back to life.

A changed boy.

Barbara replayed today's terrible exchange with her father.

"To think that I was going to make you the president next year. How am I supposed to do that now? You embarrass the Crow family name on a daily basis."

"Walter, you can still trust me. I'm sorry," pleaded Barbara. "I'll always come to you before I make any decision. Put me in charge."

"I don't know. Before today, I thought you had a brain. Now I'm wondering if I shouldn't go ahead and put your brother in charge. At least Obadiah can follow simple instructions."

"Father---"

"General Crow."

"My apologies. Please, *General Crow.* Let me prove myself to you."

"Prove to me you're not as slow as your brother? You know I only fathered one idiot, Barbara." Walter had looked at her with disgust. "The other one you created."

If only she could turn back the hands of time. Go back to when she was her daddy's little Barbie. It had been so long since he'd called her that. If only she could step into some sort of time machine. Go back to when everything was perfect. Before the accident at the boathouse.

Oh no!

The man across the park had left his bench and was heading in her direction.

Go away. Leave me alone.

The stranger stopped in front of her. "Looks like I have some competition for the saddest person in the park award."

"I think it's safe to say I'm the clear winner."

He passed her a tissue. "Joseph Carter."

She accepted it. "Thank you. Pleasure to meet you. I'm---"

"No need," he interrupted. "I know who you are."

"Please, sit."

She enjoyed his company at first. It was nice to have someone *be nice* to her. But after a few minutes, all she really wanted was to be alone.

Barbara tried her best to pay attention to what he was saying. Caught bits and pieces. Joseph was a doctor. Earlier that day, he had been fired from Light City Memorial Hospital, where he had recently been promoted to Head of the Research Department. Something to do with performing tests without approval.

She couldn't focus.

Barbara kept hearing her father's words on repeat. *I only fathered one idiot.* She worked so hard to learn everything she needed to one day take over the presidency. It was her dream to rule Barsicon with her father by her side.

Now, he thought she was too stupid to take over. What could she possibly do to prove him wrong?

"...so that is why I'm here today. Crying in the park. It's been years since I had a good cry. Felt pretty good. Miss Crow?"

Shoot! What had he been rambling on about? Something about losing his job at the hospital.

"I'm sorry that happened," she sympathized. "I'm sure you'll land on your feet."

"Probably not anytime soon. Who's going to hire me after they discover the content of my experiments? Anyway, truth be told, it was all worth it."

"How so?"

"If I wasn't fired today, I never would have met you."

The doctor had a look of love in his eyes. She couldn't remember the last time someone looked at her that way. She felt unwanted by everyone around her. Except Obadiah. The one person who loved her. Even though he had every right to hate her. If only she could go back.

Sadly, time didn't work in reverse.

"What did you say?" Joseph asked quizzically.

"I didn't say anything."

"Just now. You said time doesn't work in reverse. I heard you."

"Sorry, I was just thinking out loud."

"Don't apologize. It's just this whole time I sort of assumed you weren't paying attention."

"Sorry, I'm a bit distracted today. Tell me again what you were testing."

The doctor echoed his story. This time, she listened intently. When he finished speaking, Barbara stood up from the bench and offered him her hand. It wasn't the only thing she offered him that day.

"Any chance I could convince you to spend some time with me?"

From the goofy expression on his face, clearly the thought delighted him.

"Come now, Joseph. I have a job for you."

CHAPTER 23

WELCOME TO HEAVEN

Sunday, July 10th, 2022

Light stung her eyes even though they were closed. Was she dead? People always spoke of a bright light after death. Perhaps this was it. There was no way she was in heaven.

Unless heaven smelled like a hospital.

Seneca heard muffled voices and squinted enough to confirm her nose's suspicion. She was definitely in a hospital. Alone in a small room and lying on an uncomfortable bed. Rephrase that. Strapped down to an uncomfortable bed.

There was movement in her peripheral vision. Was the door handle actually turning or was she hallucinating?

Instinctively, she feigned sleep.

Footsteps entered the room and came to an abrupt halt at her bedside.

"Seneca." An unfamiliar man whispered her name. "It's okay to open your eyes. You're safe."

How exactly does one feel safe when strapped down?

The man touched her hand and she recoiled. It was a reminder of the restraints that confined her to a glorified gurney.

"Seneca, we know you're awake and we're here to help you."

There were others nearby. She could sense them now.

"My name is Doctor Joseph Carter. Seneca, can you hear me? You're safe and being cared for by a world-renowned medical team. Best of all, you're alive."

Seneca could hear the smile in his voice. He genuinely seemed happy she was alive. She'd give him that. But why was she still alive after being engulfed by black smoke? How much time had passed since the Light Ceremony?

If she wanted answers, she would have to concede. Return to the land of the living. Her eyes snapped open, taking the doctor by surprise.

His eyebrows lifted clear across his forehead and nearly touched his perfect hairline. "Welcome back!"

Joseph Carter was handsome. A middle-aged white man with thick, black hair and a smile that lit up the room. Likely the result of numerous dental surgeries. She couldn't take her eyes off of his colossal grin. His chompers took up half his face. His teeth were so white they illuminated the room. It wouldn't surprise her if the doctor's smile had been the bright light that woke her.

"Where am I? Why am I being restrained?"

Exhausted and scared, she forced herself to regain control. Catherine's voice ran through her head. Breathing techniques helped steady her heartbeat.

"Excellent, yes. Breathe and I'll explain everything. Like I said, my name is Doctor Joseph Carter. Please call me Dr. Joe. The most important thing to know right now is that you're safe. Okay?"

Seneca didn't feel safe. She wanted out of there. Pronto. Without use of her arms and legs, her escape options were limited.

If she could convince the doctor and his friends in the shadows to leave the room, she was confident she could unravel the polypropylene rope that tightly bound her wrists and ankles. They had been foolish enough to use a basic timber hitch knot. A toddler could work their way through that knot after breakfast and still have plenty of playtime before lunch.

She identified footsteps from three different pairs of shoes. Running shoes, women's heels and work boots. There were at least three people in the room, so her odds of escaping weren't great. Plus, she was tied down to a hospital bed.

Fight and flight were off the table.

For the first time since she'd opened her eyes, she took her gaze around the room to count her potential attackers. Her initial guess had been correct. There were three in total.

In this room anyway.

Dr. Joe was to her left. The proud owner of bright, white sneakers. Two unknowns graced her right.

The man had a blonde brush cut and was dressed in black military fatigues. He was clearly packing a 9mm in his right holster. Seneca was certain he had several other weapons hidden across his massive body. She spent longer than necessary trying to spot his neck through his muscles with limited success.

This dude was all head and shoulders.

Beside 'No Neck' was a woman who appeared to be in her mid-thirties. Her hair was the colour of a pumpkin and fell just above the name tag pinned over her heart that read 'Mary'. She wore a traditional nursing uniform, but with a small top for her tiny upper body, and a skirt one size larger to fit her backside. If she was even five feet tall it was because of the heels.

"Seneca, I would like you to meet Nurse Mary. The two of us will be taking care of your physical needs."

Really? There was a Mary and a Joseph here? Maybe she was in heaven after all. The Christian version of the afterlife. Maybe 'No Neck's' real name was Jesus and he'd spent the past two thousand and twenty-two years getting jacked.

Or perhaps after everything she had been through the past few days, she was finally starting to lose it.

Dr. Joe barked an order at his burly associate.

"Kevin!"

Kevin? Huh. Not what she was expecting.

Dr. Joe didn't bother to introduce Kevin. He simply shouted his name and ordered him to remove her restraints. Seneca eyed the doctor closely.

"Untie her at once!" he said.

Those were his words. His eyes said something else. Something more along the lines of, "Stay close. She's dangerous".

Smart man.

CHAPTER 24

SENECA'S NEW NORMAL

Now that her hands were free, Seneca was feeling more confident about defending herself, should it come to that.

That wasn't the current mood.

Kevin untied her feet and returned to the head of the bed. He stood next to Nurse Mary, who was holding a syringe full of mystery liquid.

Defending herself against me.

"Now that you've regained consciousness, you don't have to stay in this room," said Dr. Joe. "On one condition. No funny stuff. Give me a few minutes to fill you in on where you are and why you're here. Then you can be on your way."

"I can just leave?"

"Yes." He placed some clothes on the bed near her feet. "Get dressed and we'll meet you in the hallway when you're ready."

Dr. Joe flashed Seneca a smile worthy of a magazine cover and leaned down to whisper in her ear. "Have a little faith, young Light Seeker. Perhaps you've already found the light."

Seneca waited for the door to close behind them and then squeezed herself into a small bathroom.

Damn! No windows.

The clothes provided to her were a pair of camouflage pants, a black t-shirt and combat boots.

At least they knew her style.

Darting her eyes in every direction, she scanned the room for potential weapons. The mirror might be her best bet.

Realistically, what were the odds these people would save her life just so they could kill her? That scenario made no sense. They had cleaned and bandaged her wounds. She was alive because of them. Plus, they said she was free to go after their talk. How horrible could their intentions be?

Seneca wrapped her new t-shirt around her right hand and leaned into her reflection.

Crack.

One could never be too cautious.

Nurse Mary was nowhere in sight when Seneca opened the hospital room door and slipped into the hallway. Dr. Joe was there, flashing around one of his signature grins. Kevin lingered a few feet away. The man with no neck made zero effort to hide the fact that he was keeping a close eye on her.

There were also two newbies in the mix.

Seneca took stock.

The man was good-looking. He appeared to be in his late thirties or early forties with light brown skin and hair a few shades darker. His hazel eyes seemed genuinely kind. As did the big baby blues that belonged to the woman next to him.

If forced to guess, Seneca would say the woman had already celebrated her 70th birthday and that the party had been one for the history books. She wore a long, flowing skirt that was made up of every colour in existence. The world's best lion tamer couldn't control her mane. It was strewn with streaks of black and white. Each strand appeared as though it was desperately attempting to escape its owner. Her youthful eyes told the tale of a woman who had seen many things yet had not allowed the dark aspects of life to creep in and damage her spirit.

"Seneca, I would like you to meet David and Sophia. Our official welcoming committee. They're here to help you transition into your new normal."

New normal?

They shook hands. David's were clean but calloused from some sort of manual labour. Sophia's were soft to the touch. Seneca felt like she was shaking a cloud that had five feathers attached to it.

Dr. Joe led the group down the hallway to the last room on the right. He used his thumbprint to unlock the door. The room was practically empty.

Nothing to steal in here. Why lock people out? *Unless the locks were there to keep people…*

"After you," he said and held the door open for her.

Dr. Joe flipped the switch and unnatural light filled the room. The others waited in the hallway.

Seneca was alone with the doctor for the first time.

A wooden table took up most of the boardroom. It was a near duplicate of the table in the Waiting Room. The same table she sat at with her moms before the Light Ceremony. How much time had passed since then?

The room was vacant apart from the table, a few chairs and a television.

Dr. Joe sat down and motioned for her to do the same. "Please, sit. Make yourself comfortable."

Seneca sat at the head of the table.

A feeble attempt to assert herself.

There was a wall of black curtains behind the television. Seneca could tell from the rays of natural light that shone along the floor that it was a glass wall.

A window to the outside world.

She resisted the urge to run over, throw the curtains back and get a good look for herself. For now, she would practice restraint. Listen to what Dr. Joe had to say before making a bold move.

After all, she was curious to find out why she was here.

And where 'here' was.

Why had they rescued her from certain death? A nagging feeling pricked at the tip of her consciousness. Coming and going like an unfaithful spouse.

Dr. Joe picked up a remote control and flicked on the television. Apparently, there was going to be a presentation.

"At this point in the journey, most of our new community members feel a bit unnerved. We find people transition best when they watch this short video." He aimed the remote at the television. "Hopefully it answers most of your questions. If not, I'm here and I'm an open book."

Dr. Joe powered on the tube and a breathtaking photo of an island appeared on the screen. "Some people have many questions. Others have none. When the video finishes, you may ask away!"

She was no longer paying attention to him. Seneca was completely taken in by an image on the screen of a tropical island.

The picture was taken from above. Perhaps it was captured from the helicopter Seneca spotted regularly during family sailing trips along the Fennell River. The island was surrounded by white sand beaches. It was covered in hundreds of different species of plants and trees, and there was so much sun!

The waves in the once still photo began to ebb and flow. Tall trees swayed gently in the wind. A few structures came into view. Then people. The camera zoomed in and Seneca could see their smiling faces.

Four words gradually materialized across the screen.

Welcome to Heaven Island.

So this was heaven.

For the next twenty minutes, Seneca listened intently as the video played on. It described how Heaven Island came to be and what that meant for her now that she was here.

When it was over, Dr. Joe fingered the remote and paused the video on the photo of the island that had first appeared. By the end of the presentation, the frozen aerial image was less inviting.

The video was meant to calm her, but it had the opposite effect.

"Any questions, Seneca?"

Many. She shook her head and smiled at Dr. Joe, attempting to alleviate any lingering fears he may have about her being on board with this new life on Heaven Island. Assuming that's where she really was.

"Your video contains a lot of new information," she said. "It will take me some time to process."

"Yes, of course. Take as much as you need."

"I assume if I have any questions, I can ask another time?"

The doctor furrowed his brow and shifted in his seat. Even though he had presented 'no questions' as a choice, Seneca guessed not many had taken him up on that option.

"Absolutely! No problem at all. Any questions, please don't hesitate to come find me."

Seneca stood to leave. Time to test the doctor. See how serious he was about allowing her to walk away.

"One last thing."

Here we go.

"I'd like you to stop by the hospital tomorrow after lunch for a quick checkup. Standard protocol for all of our new community members."

Of course she would be seeing the doctor again. Next time, she would have more control over their meeting. For now, she decided to lay it on thick.

"I guess I owe you a huge thanks for saving my life. Heaven Island seems incredible."

"I'm so glad you feel that way." He relaxed. "I can tell that you're a smart, capable young woman. You wouldn't have made it to the seventh step without great intelligence and physical strength."

Would he always be suspicious of her? Seneca put her hands in her pockets to appear powerless. Her right thumb pressed against the smooth surface of her new pocket mirror.

"Just remember, we believe you are a good person," said Dr. Joe. "The black smoke that came close to ending your life, that was not the God of Light. We don't believe that here. I think the video made that clear."

"Yes, it did. Your description of my enlightenment was very... well, enlightening."

"Not everyone who comes here has an easy time adjusting. Hearing you can no longer see your loved ones pushes many over the edge. Just know that with each day that goes by, survivors grow to understand what a gift it is to be here. You are now among those incredible survivors."

Dr. Joe went on to explain how each community member goes through stages of shock and denial. Pain and guilt. Anger and bargaining. He told her nearly half of the islanders fell into a deep depression within the first month. Many chose to take their own lives before giving it a chance.

Some even tried to swim away.

Then, there were those who made lemonade.

"Get to know the long-term residents here, Seneca. They all started out just like you. Victims of circumstance. But they survived and found a way to thrive here. Folks like David and Sophia. You're in the best of hands with them."

They joined her hosts in the hallway.

Kevin handed Dr. Joe a walkie-talkie, similar to the ones JD would take apart back home.

Home.

Seneca was anxious to get a look at her new one, as they started down the hall towards the main entrance.

She'd been enticed from a loving place in The Darkness with stories of greatness and destiny. Stories that put pressure on her to perform and far outweighed any recent ideas she had about her life.

A life with Alex.

Then she nearly died and woke up on an island full of strangers, who she recently discovered were past Light Seekers. Alive and well despite being dead to the world.

That was her now.

16-year-old Seneca Ellis-Brant.

Dead to the world.

What pain Ma Marie and Mama C must be going through, believing she was gone. Was their sadness overshadowed by their disappointment in her failure? Were they angry their dreams of living in Light City had gone up in smoke, along with their daughter?

They arrived at the main entrance. The doors swung open on their own and it took her by surprise.

Automatic doors!

She had to admit, it was exciting to see Light City technology at work.

A waft of ocean air blew across her face.

Seneca smiled. It wasn't the salty ocean breeze or the stunning scenery that made her beam. It was the new goal she had set for herself.

To learn everything about this place so she could escape and see her family again.

Automatic doors be damned.

Seneca had often wondered what would come next for her after the Light Ceremony. She had imagined herself dancing in expensive suits on an oceanfront balcony, while chefs prepared feasts of ribs and more ribs.

That was no longer her destiny.

A new mission formed in her mind.

It wouldn't be easy. She would have to train alone. Figure out the steps without any actual steps to follow.

Finding allies would be difficult. It took time to earn trust.

She had trusted when Alex told her she wouldn't die because of an innocent kiss. Look how that turned out.

But she wasn't dead.

She was very much alive and ready to plan her escape.

This journey would require her to learn new skills. Seneca had already convinced Dr. Joe that she was okay with living on the island for the rest of her life, no questions asked. Yet she wasn't taught manipulation as a Light Seeker.

Although she had witnessed that trait in certain folks in the village.

Catherine called them 'hustlers' and said they used their words to get whatever they wanted, with no concern for the truth.

Seneca practiced at home one day on her dolls, trying to convince Nina to give her three apples for the price of two. She had promised the doll extra speaking time during afternoon tea, then didn't give it to her, too excited about her first sail on Fee Fee earlier in the day. On and on she rambled, giving no extra time to raggedy ol' Nina.

Was that the reason the black smoke had overcome her?

Nothing else came to mind. She had been nearly perfect her entire life. Certainly, hustling dolls wasn't a good enough reason for the God of Light to condemn your soul to eternal damnation.

Death had inched close once before and she wouldn't let it get that close again. Survival was at her core and every fibre of her being warned her this was a case of survival.

No, this new journey would not be easy. It appeared she was destined to navigate it solo. But she was determined to get off this island and find her moms.

Or die trying.

CHAPTER 25

CATHERINE AND MARIE SET SAIL

Even if they died trying, Marie and Catherine were determined to set sail in the West Ocean and find Seneca.

After a stagnant fifteen hours, her tracker was showing slight movement again and Catherine was no longer biting the skin from the sides of her fingernails. Any longer and Marie worried she might start biting her actual nails.

A definite first for the Princess of The Darkness.

Satisfied they had everything they needed to cast off, Marie grabbed a map from the table in the galley and traced their course.

If the winds co-operated, it would take almost two days to reach her.

Assuming Seneca stayed where she was.

Besides open water, there wasn't much between their launching point on the Fennell River and the spot where she hovered mysteriously over the West Ocean. Marie guessed Seneca was on a boat that had anchored for the night. Or she could be on one of the ghost islands, unmarked on any map.

Marie didn't wish to entertain any other options.

Even though she knew their supplies were in order, she checked them again. They couldn't afford to run into any trouble. Fresh water. Check. Fuel and batteries. Check, check. It was all there, weapons included, thanks to JD.

She closed the forward hatches.

It was almost time to set sail.

Days before the Light Ceremony, she had tried to stop it from happening, but Catherine wouldn't have it. Her faith in Seneca's destiny was infallible.

Marie was also a believer. A believer in inserting a tracker inside the girl's leg when she was a child so they wouldn't lose her. Neither woman knew what happened to a person after they 'died' during their Light Ceremony, but they knew they weren't all dead. They couldn't be.

Seneca was on the move.

That was proof enough that they had done the right thing. They were *doing* the right thing. So why was she still having reservations?

Maybe because they hadn't told Seneca the entire truth from the beginning. They assumed she couldn't handle it.

In hindsight, the truth would have been much easier.

Following the Light Ceremony, they'd been overwhelmed by well-intentioned people extending their condolences. Who in their right mind thinks a grieving parent wants to talk to a stranger minutes after their child dies? *About their death!*

"We all thought she'd make it. Did you have any doubts?"

"Witnessing the smoke turn black must have been horrifying for you."

"Sorry you won't be living in Light City, Catherine. I know you really wanted to move back."

By the time they made it home, Seneca could have been taken by boat or helicopter to a ghost island.

There were rumours of massive plots of land in the West Ocean controlled by the Crow family. Marie and Catherine had no doubt the Crows were behind whatever was happening beyond the Light Ceremonies.

As soon as they found their daughter, they would be able to prove it.

Weather was their biggest concern. Forecasters were calling for a major storm on Tuesday. If they didn't make it to Seneca before then, they would need to change course and take cover on land.

Marie had built Fee Fee and knew the boat's limitations. If the storm was bad, there was no way she could ride it out safely.

"Catherine!" she called from the galley. "It's almost time to set sail. What kind of winds are we looking at?"

"Southwest, 15 knots. Casting off shouldn't be a problem. We might encounter some strong headwinds later tonight."

Marie climbed companionway to the deck. "Might require a little bit of tacking, but we'll be okay."

"Looks like we're all set, Captain."

Growing up in Light City, Catherine had sailed along the West Ocean many times. Until now, it had only been a dream for Marie.

A dream that was about to become a reality.

She was excited to feel the power of the ocean. Fee Fee might be able to reach eight or nine knots with the wind on the beam.

However, anxiety dimmed her excitement.

What shape would Seneca be in when they found her? At least they knew she was still alive and they had her location. That knowledge gave both women hope, as they set out to save their daughter and quell the ghosts of their past.

CHAPTER 26

THE IMPATIENT PRESIDENT

What was taking him so long?

"Slow Joe," Barbara muttered to herself in the bathroom mirror.

She applied the final touches of her dark red lipstick. If only the good doctor would get a goddamn move on it! She refused to be late for brunch at Crow Castle.

Barbara stared at herself in the mirror. She hated visits to this dreaded island. As soon as Joseph finished the experiments, she could stop hanging out in this hospital and start living the life she'd been working towards for decades.

It wouldn't be so bad if she could explore the island. Enjoy the outdoors from someplace other than the rooftop patio.

That was far too risky though. Someone might see her. That would put the entire project in jeopardy.

The most recent experiments had been yielding favourable results. But until the technology was perfected, this was her reality.

Hopefully, not for much longer.

Barbara's patience was wearing thin. Joseph had noticed and was working eighteen-hour days.

Success was within reach.

The sooner they achieved their goal, the sooner they could leave this island behind forever.

At least she had made her space bearable.

Barbara had converted the entire top floor of the hospital into a lavish penthouse. All four walls were floor to ceiling windows with rounded corners for a smooth, 360-degree view of the West Ocean. Priceless works of art hung on the walls. Sculptures handcrafted by the masters were on display.

Still, despite all the beauty around her, Barbara was irritated. Where was Joseph? Probably in that girl's room being his kind, slothful self. Always so nice and always so slow. Two of many things she detested about him.

Her anxiety levels were peaking. How hard was it to wake the kid up and hand her off to the welcoming committee?

"I'm not getting any younger here." Barbara inspected for new wrinkles around her mouth.

Not yet anyway.

CHAPTER 27

THE BEACH HOUSE

The video didn't do the island justice. It was even more spectacular in real life. The colours, more vibrant. The people, happier.

David and Sophia lived a short walk from the hospital. Good thing because she was feeling a bit woozy. Walking seemed to be the only mode of transportation anyway. Not a car or truck in sight.

A helicopter rested on the roof of the hospital.

It was hard to miss.

The hospital sat on higher ground, at the northeastern tip of Heaven Island. It was a slight downhill walk to the other buildings, mostly houses.

Log cabins!

"Well, this is it. The beach house. Home sweet home," said David, holding open the door. "Why don't I make us a snack while Sophia shows you to your room?"

The log cabin was remarkably similar to the one she grew up in. Complete with a wraparound porch.

Except the backyard was an ocean.

And it was so bright inside!

Twice as many windows meant twice as much light. It was almost as bright inside the house as it was outside.

"The mattress is a twin, but it's fit for a queen," said Sophia. "Super comfy. I washed all of the bedding yesterday, just in case.

We never know if someone is going to show up after the Light Ceremony."

"How long have you been here?"

Sophia gave her a resigned smile. "A long time, babe."

"Will you tell me about your Light Ceremony?"

"Sure. Why don't you take a moment to settle in. Then I'll tell you all about it. I'm sure David will too."

"Thanks. I have so many questions. Especially after watching that video."

"That stupid video! I told Dr. Joe that it freaks people out, but do you think he listens? *Noooo.* All hair and teeth, that one."

Seneca laughed for the first time since arriving on the island and decided right away that she liked this woman, with her wild gray streaks and colourful clothes. Quite the character. Such a youthful spirit for someone who must be in her seventies.

"Okay, babe. You'll notice there are clothes in the drawers that were dropped off for you earlier and maybe an item or two that they thought you might enjoy. Snoop around and join us in the kitchen for a bite when you're ready."

"Thank you so much. I really appreciate your kindness."

"That's all you'll ever get from me. Love and kindness are my two fortés. Painting is my third. I'll show you my studio after lunch."

And with that, she was gone.

Seneca looked around the bedroom. She liked it. It was cozy, and it would serve its purpose for a few nights.

Mainly blue and white, there was clearly a nautical theme. The dark blue bedspread was covered in tiny white sailboats. Decorative ropes hung from the ceiling. Paintings of lighthouses and anchors covered almost every square inch of wall space.

Even the knobs on the three dresser drawers were tiny helms.

The top drawer was filled with socks, underwear and t-shirts. The middle drawer was packed full of shorts, pants and a couple of sweaters. The bottom drawer was twice the size of the others, but she couldn't open it. It was jammed.

Jammed or locked?

She would look into it later. Right now, she needed to eat something.

Before she joined David and Sophia in the kitchen, she poked her head inside the bedroom closet. A shoe rack held a few pairs of sandals, running shoes and boots. All her size and style.

The best part? *Bookshelves!* All three walls were lined with paperbacks and hardcovers. Fiction and nonfiction. Mysteries. Romances. Autobiographies. Historical and horror, as well as comedy and fantasy novels.

For the first time since she arrived on Heaven Island, for a brief moment she actually felt like she was in heaven.

David's snack was more of a meal. Seneca was stuffed by the time they finished the spread of meats, cheeses, fruits, vegetables and homemade desserts. Her new host was quite the baker. She filled her stomach with sweet treats: butter tarts, macarons and crème brûlée.

Three strawberries covered in dark chocolate disappeared as soon as she discovered them. Whoever invented that combination was a genius!

Over lunch, Seneca kept the conversation light. David and Sophia were clearly happy with the life they had built here, and she didn't want them to think she was desperately trying to run away from them.

Even though she was.

Without too much prodding, she managed to uncover a bit about their lives on the island.

Sophia was among the first to arrive in 2003. David followed two years later. There were three other Light Seekers living on Heaven Island when she touched down, plus Dr. Joe and Kevin. Nurse Mary and the others showed up later. More Light Seekers were saved and additional staff were hired to take care of them.

Kitchen staff ran the cafeteria at breakfast and the dining hall at dinner. At lunchtime you had to fend for yourself.

Seneca didn't anticipate that being a problem with David around.

There were cleaners that came into every home twice a week to tidy up. Whether they were needed or not. Seneca assumed they had just finished a deep clean before she arrived, until Sophia mentioned they should get out of the house to give the cleaner some privacy.

"Wanna check out my studio, babe?"

"I'd love to!"

She followed Sophia to a shed off the side of the house. The building had its own spectacular view of the West Ocean.

On the deck next to them, David sprawled out on his lounger.

"He's obsessed with reading. Sometimes he gets his nose in a book after lunch and I have to beg him to put it down so we can go to dinner. If you're a reader, there's no shortage of books around here to enjoy."

"That's amazing. I do love to read."

"You're in the right place."

Sophia pushed the shed door open with her hip. "Après vous, mademoiselle."

"I like 'babe' better," she joked.

"*Ha!*" Sophia ushered her into the studio. "I like you. Babe it is."

The studio was a sensory overload. Sophia's talent was obvious. Her style, less-so. Her paintings ranged from abstract to surrealism. Modernism to impressionism. Seneca had studied art and saw examples of cubism, futurism and pop art. There were oils, acrylics and pastels.

"Are all of these yours?"

"Every last one of them. My babies."

"They're beautiful."

"Thank you. I birthed them myself."

"I hope the labour wasn't too difficult."

"No, the labour was the fun part. It's the delivery that's tough for me."

Sophia explained that most of the art was hers that hung on the walls of island homes, and while she was happy to use her artistic skills to beautify the blank spaces, it was always hard to say goodbye. The artwork in the studio were the pieces she refused to give away.

"Some things you just don't part ways with," she told Seneca. "Do you have anything like that?"

"Not really. At one time, maybe. A book that I gave away."

"You must've given it to someone special."

"I did."

Alex.

Seneca missed them so much. How were they feeling about her being a failed Light Seeker? She hoped they didn't feel responsible. Shared kisses couldn't be to blame for the smoke turning black.

Or could they?

Maybe Seneca was not as pure as she was supposed to be.

Stop that!

With a baptism under three minutes, she couldn't be that impure. Besides, now was not the time for feelings of guilt and shame.

So what if she hadn't made it to Light City.

Now she was in heaven.

Right?

"We hate to interrupt whatever epic saga you've thrown yourself into today, but how about a walk down the beach?"

"Sure, Sophia." David lifted himself from his lounger. "Seneca, are you feeling up to it?"

"Absolutely. Your lunch gave me plenty of fuel. Maybe too much! Probably smart to walk it off."

The sand was warm and soft on her bare feet. A stark contrast to the wet grass she was accustomed to running through or the scorching concrete that hardened her soles. The ocean had been calling to her from the moment she walked through the hospital's automatic doors.

Seneca stuck her toes in the water. "This might be hard for both of you to believe, but I've never been in the ocean before."

Sophia looked genuinely shocked. "Child, what? My lord. Get in there!"

"Sophia, why don't you grab a bathing suit for Seneca from---"

Before David could finish his sentence, the older woman grabbed her hand and was pulling her towards the West Ocean.

They ran into the water together.

Laughing.

Splashing.

Seneca dove down and touched the sand at her feet. A few strokes underwater and then she resurfaced. Refreshing was an understatement. Salt saturated her lips. She stood in waist deep water, closed her eyes and lifted her face to the sky, basking in the hot sun overhead.

"I think she likes the ocean."

"I'd say so." David stood along the shoreline with his pants rolled up to his knees. "Next time, why don't you bring some towels. Maybe throw on a bathing suit."

"Mr. Serious Planner. Whatever would we do without you?"

Sophia swiped her hand across the water's edge. A few ocean droplets made their way onto David's khakis.

"You wouldn't know today is Wednesday if it wasn't for me."

"Yes, I would!" said Sophia.

David laughed. "Exactly. It's Sunday, *'babe'*."

Jokes and jabs aside, Seneca could feel the love between the two of them. Whatever their relationship was, it was a special bond.

Soaking wet, they skipped the rest of their walk and set up on the beach close to home. She sat in the sand with Sophia. David perched himself on a nearby log.

They listened to the sounds of the birds and the waves lapping against the shoreline. With help from the hot sun, their clothes dried in no time. She was able to brush the sand off easily by the time they headed back to the log cabin.

Before that, Seneca was able to do some digging.

"Sophia, it's fascinating that you were one of the first to arrive. Was any of this even built at the time?"

"The hospital was here and a couple of buildings that have since been torn down. Whoever was responsible for building the homes before David didn't have the skills he possesses."

"You built the homes here?"

"The log cabins. I've been here since 2005. Needed something to keep me busy."

"It's been a few years since David's had to build a new one," said Sophia. "I'm pretty sure they thought we would all want our own homes, but not many live alone around here. Most are happy for the company."

"Is that why you two live together?" she asked.

"We enjoy each other's company," David replied.

"Plus, we share a common bond. We both drowned on the fifth step."

"Really? Please tell me more about how you ended up here."

For the next hour, she was captivated by their stories. Both David and Sophia described being inside the baptism tank. The struggle to hold their breath. The feeling of defeat when they finally let go.

Unlike Seneca, they remembered the trip to Heaven Island. Dr. Joe revived them in the back of an ambulance, while Kevin drove them to a secluded spot where they were loaded into a helicopter.

Long before the welcome video was ever produced.

According to Sophia, there were three other Light Seekers on the island when she first arrived who were long gone now. Seneca was quite sure she knew what 'long gone' meant.

David landed on the island two years after Sophia. Shortly after his arrival, all new island residents were sedated for the journey. Her new hosts agreed that if given the option, they would have loved to be 'out' for the ride.

Seneca wouldn't be surprised if it had been them who suggested sedation to Dr. Joe in the first place.

They certainly championed it.

Especially Sophia. "They could give me a little needle poke right now. Put me out for the night. Wouldn't bother me any!"

The cackle that followed made Seneca laugh. She really liked her. However, there was one thing about her story she couldn't quite put together.

"Sophia, how old were you when you attempted the Seven Steps into the Light?"

The question caught her off-guard. "Uhhhh geez, babe. I don't even remember now. Old. Probably the oldest!"

"I thought the oldest Light Seeker was fifty. You must have been in your fifties if your ceremony was nineteen years ago?"

"Close. I was 48 years old. Guess the island sun has damaged my skin more than I care to admit."

Seneca felt stupid for asking and quickly turned to David. "How old were you when you attempted it?"

"Twenty-three. Man, I really thought I had it too. Then the seconds underwater turned into minutes. Minutes turned into darkness, and well...you know the rest."

"The fifth step scared me the most. I used to have nightmares about it all the time," she admitted.

"I still have nightmares about it," said Sophia. "How long were you under?"

"Two minutes and forty-seven seconds."

"Precious, babe. Good on ya."

"Thanks. I was doing really well until I stepped into that glass box on the seventh step."

David looked at her with sympathetic eyes. "Let me guess. Black smoke and then the floor dropped out?"

"Not the first, eh?"

"Nope. And if I were a betting man, I'd put money down that you won't be the last."

Dinner was still two hours away when David suggested she lie down for a nap. A brilliant idea considering the sedation she'd been given the night before. The drugs, combined with the hot sun, topped off what was already an emotional twenty-four hours.

"Rest up, babe. We'll come wake you when it's time to go to the dining hall."

Seneca considered changing into some fresh clothes. Exhaustion won out. Most of the sand had fallen off of her on their walk back to the beach house anyway. Plus, she wasn't about to get under the blankets. It was too warm for that.

She collapsed on top of the comforter and stared at the ceiling fan.

What a day it had been already and it was still far from over. The afternoon with David and Sophia had been so entertaining, she had almost forgotten about the video. About being told that she could never see her family again.

Maybe it wasn't getting to her because she was still in shock?

Or maybe it was because she didn't believe a word that came out of Dr. Joe's mouth.

Deep down, she knew she would see her family again. In a way, she sensed they were already there with her.

Eyelids heavy, muscles relaxed, she felt herself drift away. Near-sleep, she rolled onto her side and was jolted awake by a sharp pain in her upper thigh.

The shard of glass from the hospital mirror was still in her pocket.

Seneca had forgotten all about it.

CHAPTER 28

DINNER IS SERVED

Never in her life was she watched so closely while she ate. From the moment she entered the room, all eyes were on her.

Fresh meat.

The dining hall was exquisite. Lights dimmed. Candles lit. The white napkins and tablecloths were spotless. A quick head count told her there were about eighty people living on the island, assuming everyone was here. Who would miss dinner? It was even more extravagant than David's lunchtime snack.

She was offered meat, fish and vegetarian options.

Seneca said yes to all three.

Halfway through the second plate, she started to slow. By the third serving, she was finally speaking between bites.

"Is that Jax in the corner with those three women?"

"Sure is. All these years later, the poor babe still misses his mama. He's always hanging around with those old broads. Lookin' for some lovin'."

David turned fifty shades of red. "Sophia!"

"It's true! Remember when the kid first showed up? He followed me around for days trying to latch on to these teats."

"Enough," pleaded David. "How about some dessert?"

Three plates of dinner were ample for Seneca. She remained seated at the table and observed her surroundings.

Specifically, she observed Jax.

Before Seneca, Jax was the youngest Light Seeker. That was over a decade ago. He would be close to thirty now. If Dr. Joe had a son, Jax could be him. Same dark hair and perfect smile. Both good-looking men and well aware of it.

As a young girl, she had watched his Light Ceremony and still remembered the moment of his 'death'. The Northern Warrior had cheated. Weapons were not allowed. Yet the warrior had pulled a sword out of his leather kilt and slit Jax's throat while the crowd cheered on.

Jax noticed her ogling him.

The thick scar across the front of his neck became more obvious as he stepped into close range and sat down next to her.

"You know it's rude to stare."

"Oh, I know." Seneca surveyed the room. "That's exactly what I've been thinking this entire dinner."

"Everyone wants to get a good look at the newbie. Can't blame them really. But what's your excuse?" asked Jax, with a wink and a seductive smile. "See something you like?"

Perhaps he didn't realize she was sixteen. "Yes, I do. I like the look of those women sitting at your table. Guess I miss my moms."

A glimpse of acknowledgement in his eyes.

"Two days ago, I was celebrating my sixteenth birthday with them. Now I'm here."

"On an island full of misfits."

"It appears that way."

"Sixteen, eh? Sorry about, errr, well whatever. Sorry for being so forward."

The flirting stopped, but the conversation about her age didn't. It was still a big deal to Jax. Until Seneca came along, he had carried the distinction of being the youngest Light Seeker.

"So how many steps did you make it through before...you know," he trailed off.

"All the way to the seventh," she replied.

"No way! Damn, wish I'd made it there." Was Jax aware that he was holding his throat? "Suppose I'm just happy I made it here. From what they tell me, it was touch and go for a bit."

After a few minutes of idle chit chat with Jax, who was less obnoxious than she expected him to be, David and Sophia returned with four plates of dessert.

"Oh, no. I couldn't take another bite if I wanted to," said Seneca.

"That is very nice, but I should get back to my table," added Jax.

Sophia laughed. "You two think these are for you?"

Her wild hair brushed David's shoulder, as she looked back and forth between the plates in his hands, and the two portions she was holding.

"David, were you planning on sharing your desserts?"

He looked at his roommate with a stern expression. "Not a chance."

"*Okay!* Seneca is new here, but I should've known better," said Jax. "Catch you folks later. Are you going to the bonfire tomorrow night?"

"Assuming the rain holds off," said David. "I overheard some of the security guards talking about a big storm moving in early Tuesday."

"Cool. Well, maybe I'll see y'all there."

CHAPTER 29

A LIGHT SEEKER NAMED MICAH

Most of Sophia's artwork was in her studio, but her bedroom was a work of art unto itself. Seneca was surprised to see every inch of wall space covered in a beach scene.

"Having the beach outside your backdoor isn't enough?"

"You kill me, babe."

She pointed to the wall beside Sophia's bed. "Who's that?"

There were several people painted into the mural. One stood out among the rest. The man was a few feet taller than everyone else. His head was topped with long, dark dreadlocks. Tattoos covered his muscular arms and chest. He wore a stern expression on his angular face.

Despite his aggressive physical appearance, his gray eyes shone bright with love and light. Seneca could feel his good vibes through Sophia's painted expression of the man, who was...a Northern Warrior? The size almost matched, but he was missing the signature ringed beard.

"That is Micah. One of the best humans to ever grace this big, beautiful planet."

"Is he a Barsiconian or a Northern Warrior?"

"Both."

"Both? But how..."

She had never heard of such a thing. Northern Warriors were a different species all together. Weren't they?

"Where is he now?"

"That is a really good question. He's not on the island anymore. Trust me, I searched high and low."

"How long ago was that?"

"Over a decade ago now."

Micah arrived in 2004. One year after Sophia, and one year before David. Back then, they all lived together in one building. They slept in a shared room full of bunk beds in what was now the cafeteria.

David snuck up behind them. "I miss that guy."

"Oh, hey there. I was just telling Seneca about Micah. I miss him, too."

"It was certainly much harder to build log cabins after he disappeared."

"Great muscle to have around. Remember how everyone thought you were being lazy because you kept disappearing from job sites?"

David laughed. "Yes! Of course. My secret project."

"You were absolutely giddy when you dragged all of us there."

Sophia explained how they had walked away from the ocean, into the woods and down a recently cut path for fifteen minutes before they arrived at the spot where David presented his surprise.

"For you, Micah. I know how much you enjoy your solitude. We built it with some extra headroom."

Under David's direction, the islanders had built a high-ceilinged home for the tall man with a kind heart. It was away from all the others, but still close enough that he felt connected. No more ducking under doorways or busting wooden chairs. Micah had his own custom-made home.

"I ran back and forth so many times when we built that place. My cardio was never better," said David.

All three stood and stared at Sophia's rendition of Micah on the wall. In a weird way, Seneca felt sad that she would never meet him. He seemed like an incredible person from the pictures Sophia had painted with her brushes and words.

"The sun is about to go down, babes. Should we watch from the beach?"

"I'd love that. David, you in?"

"Well, I did have pretty big plans tonight. But I suppose the library will still be there tomorrow morning."

A cool, comfortable breeze. They set a blanket on the sand. A tray of wine and cheese in the centre.

"How many people live on Heaven Island? I counted about eighty at dinner tonight."

"Very observant," said David. "There are probably about 100 in total. Not everyone comes to dinner."

She was dumbfounded. "How could anyone skip that feast?"

"After a few years, you don't mind missing the odd meal here and there."

"Babe, pass me that bottle of wine. Want some?"

"I've only tried it once," she admitted.

"Did you like it?"

"I didn't love the taste, but I liked the way it made me feel."

Sophia poured her a half glass and they sat back to enjoy the striking sunset. It was her first without the Crow Line obstructing her view and it was nothing short of spectacular.

The sky glowed a bright orange!

It reminded her of the orange grove. The oranges on Alex's outfit. What were they doing right now? She could only assume they were still at their cousin's house. How was JD holding up? Was he more upset about her death than Cooper's? He must be.

Seneca missed home.

This island would *not* be her new one.

"When I first arrived, Dr. Joe mentioned that some Light Seekers who were saved didn't like being here. Even took their own lives. Is that true?" she asked.

"It's true that not everyone likes being here," replied David. "Whether they took their own lives or not is a different question."

"Sophia, please don't."

"Don't what, David?"

Silence fell between the pair. She reached for David's cheese knife, hoping to cut the tension.

It only worked on the cheese.

"The girl doesn't need to worry herself with the way life used to be."

"Weren't you curious to know everything when you first arrived? We are all Light Seekers here. Survival is in our gut. Help the girl out. Stop making everything so fucking mysterious."

"Sophia, please keep your voice down."

"Why? Will the ocean come for me?"

Frizzy streaks of black and white blew in the wind, hiding Sophia's face as she pushed herself to standing. The woman brushed the hair from her eyes.

That's when she saw them.

Tears, streaming down Sophia's face.

Wet sadness pooled in the creases that lined her cheeks. Seneca swore the woman had more wrinkles now than when they'd met earlier that day.

David jumped up and embraced his friend. "Sophia, I'm sorry. I'm so sorry."

They held onto each other and watched the sun go down.

Clearly, the old woman had forgiven him.

As the sun disappeared, so did Seneca. She went back to the room full of sailing paraphernalia that reminded her of home.

The one place she longed to be.

She had to escape and make it back to her family. If she needed to, she would comb every inch of the island for clues. Dr. Joe was expecting her at the hospital tomorrow. She could pretend to get lost. Roam the halls. Maybe find herself in areas that are meant for hospital staff only.

In the meantime, she would tackle the mystery dresser. The big drawer with the tiny helm that didn't turn. Seneca surveyed the room for something small that she could use to pick the lock. She didn't see anything that would help.

If she could just get a closer look.

Down on her hands and knees, she noticed the handle didn't turn clockwise like the others. It had to be pushed.

But it's the same dresser?

Why would the mechanics on this drawer be different than the other two?

Seneca pushed the miniature steering wheel and the drawer popped out, smacking into her. It didn't hurt, or even throw her off balance, but she was taken aback.

Inside the once seemingly locked drawer was---nothing.

It was empty.

Mystery solved.

CHAPTER 30

A HOSPITAL VISIT

Monday, July 11th, 2022

When she arrived at the hospital the next day, Dr. Joe was sitting on a bench outside waiting for her. Any snooping around would have to be done after her appointment. As usual, his hair and teeth were perfectly polished.

"Seneca! Welcome back. Good to see you again."

"Hi, Dr. Joe. Beautiful day."

"Indeed! Although you may want to prepare yourself. I hear there's a big storm moving in overnight."

"Thankfully I have a beautiful log cabin to shelter me. It's just like the one I lived in back home," said Seneca, careful not to look too sad when she said the word 'home'.

"David and Sophia are wonderful hosts, aren't they?"

"Second to none."

The hospital stood ten stories high, which was about eight stories higher than it needed to be. The bottom floor was busy, but almost every other level appeared vacant.

Except the top floor.

Light shone from the tenth level last night. She had noticed it from the beach house.

When they arrived at the end of a hallway, Dr. Joe ushered Seneca into the same room where she woke up yesterday.

"Hop on the bed. Let's take a look at how you're healing."

If you promise not to restrain me this time.

Seneca had only suffered a few minor bumps and bruises during her Light Ceremony. Most of the damage was done when she fell through the floor of the glass box and into the steep hole below it. The jagged shaft had cut up the sides of her arms.

Nurse Mary came to draw blood.

'No Neck' Kevin was nowhere to be seen.

They took her blood pressure. Listened to her lungs. Dr. Joe used a wooden tongue depressor to check the back of her throat and an otoscope to get a good look inside her ears.

Satisfied that she was healthy, he told her she was free to go. "Enjoy the sunshine before it disappears!"

"Oh, I most certainly will. Might even try another ocean swim. Yesterday was the first of what I'm sure will be many refreshing dips." Seneca laid it on thicker than peanut butter. "Thanks again for making my transition here so comfortable, Dr. Joe."

"Anything else I can do, please let me know."

Then he did the *one thing* Seneca was praying he wouldn't do.

He walked her to the front door.

"See ya when I see ya."

"Yeah, see ya when I see ya," she repeated, silently wishing she wouldn't see the doctor anytime soon.

A quick glance back.

The doctor stood at the entrance with his arms crossed and waited for her to leave. Dr. Joe still considered her a threat and he was protective of whatever was going on in that hospital.

Seneca heard the sounds of the automatic doors closing behind her as she walked away, followed by the *chuff-chuff-chuff* of an approaching helicopter.

Was the helicopter the only way on and off Heaven Island?

It was impossible to tell how far she was from the mainland.

Sophia had told her tales of Light Seekers who tried to swim their way off the island. Their success was anyone's guess.

Either way, they were never heard from again.

It was a chance most people weren't willing to take.

CHAPTER 31

A PROJECT UPDATE

"Stick close," she told the pilot. "I'll be less than an hour."

Wind from the helicopter blades whipped Barbara's red hair in all directions. Someday, she would never again have to visit this dreaded island.

That day couldn't come soon enough.

President Crow descended the stairs from the roof of the hospital to the penthouse and waited for Joseph. She was always waiting for the doctor.

For twenty years now.

Luckily, this time she only had to wait twenty minutes before the elevator doors opened.

"Barbara, darling. Are you here?"

"I'm in the kitchen."

Joseph pulled Barbara into his arms, squeezed her tight and attempted a romantic kiss. A peck was all he received in return.

His extreme affection should please her. Instead, it irritated her.

Most things irritated her.

"Did it work?"

"We didn't do the experiment today. It was just a regular check-up."

"What are you waiting for Joseph? Time is running out."

"I can't just bring her into the hospital and throw her in right away. She's smart. We need to be smarter."

Barbara couldn't listen to his excuses any longer. "It doesn't work. That's the problem, isn't it? We're days away and it doesn't work."

"It works! I'll prove it to you, sweetheart. It was necessary to draw blood from the girl today to ensure we're good to go tomorrow and we are. We're ready."

"Tomorrow. You promise?"

"Yes, my love. I promise. Will you be here to watch?"

"I wouldn't miss it."

CHAPTER 32

MISSING ISLANDERS

The afternoon sun was strong. Her skin was lathered in sunscreen. Catherine would be proud. Seneca sat in a lounger on the back porch of the beach house. Her face was in a book, but she wasn't reading.

She was planning.

Outlining her escape.

The hospital visit had been a setback. The key to whatever was happening on Heaven Island was locked inside that building and she had banked on gathering more intel during her check-up today.

Doctor Handsome had made sure that didn't happen.

There was one piece of valuable information she gleaned on her walk out of the examination room. The door to the adjacent room was open and so was the window. Every other window in the hospital appeared to be sealed tight.

Not this one.

A flimsy screen was the only thing barring someone from coming in or out. The room was located on the far east side of the building. If she walked along the beach this afternoon she could get a better look.

Knock! Knock!

Seneca made her way around the wraparound porch towards the front of the house. *Wait.* This wasn't her house. She headed back to her lounge chair as David answered the door.

"Carol Morgan!" His tone softened. "Is everything okay?"

"Have you seen Nick?" The woman was frantic. "He's been missing for two days. No one has heard a peep."

Seneca paused and tuned in.

"No, I haven't seen him. I'm sure he's alright though. It's not like it's the first time he's taken off."

"It feels different this time. Like he's gone for good."

"I get it, Carol. You're like a mother to that one. But Nick likes to do what Nick likes to do."

"I know."

"Did you check Micah's old place? That's where we found him the last time he disappeared."

Carol's voice shook. "I've made the trek five times in the last twenty-four hours. The place is as empty as the day Micah disappeared."

"Our buddy Nick never misses a bonfire. Before we panic, let's see if he shows up tonight. In the meantime, get some rest. I think you need it."

Rest was on the agenda that afternoon for David and Sophia. While they napped, Seneca decided to go for a walk down the beach and get a closer look at the hospital. If she mapped out her route in the daylight, it would be easier to get there under the cover of night.

Before she stepped off the back porch, a familiar face ran up to greet her.

"Hey, stranger."

"Jax. Nice scorching day for a run."

His body dripped with sweat. Or had he just gone for a swim? She didn't know. Either way, he was drenched.

"Love my daily runs. Rain, shine or extra shine."

"I have some pent-up energy to work off. Mind if I join you?" she asked.

Jax was jogging in the direction of the hospital. Not a bad idea to have a pal with her. It was less suspicious than the new girl snooping around alone.

"Sure, you can join me," he replied. "If you think you can keep up!"

CHAPTER 33

THE BOAT RIDE TO HELL

There wasn't a cloud in the sky, but Marie knew what was coming. Fee Fee was gliding through the West Ocean. The boat was delightfully cooperative.

Even Catherine was helpful.

"Can I grab you some lunch? We have pre-made sandwiches. Or I can hand you a fork and a can of something."

"Fork me."

"I'll fork you alright!"

Marie laughed, even though she wasn't in the mood for jokes. She was focused on Seneca. Her tracker showed consistent movement in a small area.

Was she on a ghost island or a boat?

She tried her best not to think about the dangers Seneca could be facing and focused on what was in front of her.

In front, beside and behind.

The West Ocean.

Sailing Fee Fee along the Fennell River had always been fun and exciting, but there was a freedom out on the ocean that didn't translate to fresh water. Nausea was another feeling that came up often. The waves and currents were so much stronger than she was used to.

The ocean also made her feel tiny and insignificant, and at the same time, connected. The bright blues and greens left her awestruck, as did some of the creatures they encountered along the way.

Jellyfish and rays. A pod of dolphins swam alongside the boat for a short time. They were quite the entertainers! She saw manatees and a whale. Catherine spotted a shark, but Marie was using the head at the time and missed it.

Catherine tossed her a can of beans. “I’ll take the helm.”

Four hours on watch.

Four hours off.

As magical as it was to sail in the West Ocean for the first time, she couldn’t fully enjoy it. Not until her entire family was together again. Marie was determined to make that happen.

Determined and prepared.

She tossed aside the half-empty can of beans and took stock of her arsenal. Guns and ammo. Knives and explosives. They were ready. They *had* to be ready for whatever they encountered when they reached their destination.

What was their destination?

At this point, it was Seneca.

Every single day, she questioned whether they made the right decision to raise Seneca as a Light Seeker. Now it was too late for questions. They had to push ahead.

Only forward.

It was mostly guilt that propelled her. She had to make things right. Seneca was her blood.

The story of the child’s miracle birth was close to the truth. The closest they could get without complicating an already extremely complicated situation.

Surely their daughter would forgive them. Listen to their side of the story and understand her destiny was predetermined. Seneca was born to help bring the people out of the darkness and into the light.

One skewed detail didn’t change that fact.

"The winds are starting to pick up, but they're working in our favour," said Catherine. "We should be able to stay the course until the storm hits."

"Have you checked the weather radar recently?"

"About twenty minutes ago. It looks like we have eight to ten hours before the storm catches up with us."

It wasn't enough time.

"Unless Seneca's tracker miraculously moves closer to us, I'd say we are still about twelve hours away."

Catherine's shoulders lowered.

Marie tried to lift them with a smile.

She had to exude confidence, even if she wasn't feeling secure. Everyone had their role in a relationship, and when it came to the two of them, she was the pillar.

Strong and steady Marie.

No need to change course now.

CHAPTER 34

A RUN ON THE BEACH

"I take it back, Seneca. There's no way I can keep up with you!"

Jax decelerated from a slow run to a slow walk. Then he stopped and rested his hands on his thighs.

"Don't bend over. It restricts your airway."

"Thanks, genius."

"Well, according to my IQ---"

"Yeah, yeah, smarty pants."

The banter back and forth made Seneca wish she had an older brother. JD and Ernest were both important men in her life, but she imagined having a brother or father was something different.

Having David around was comforting and having a strong-minded woman like Sophia nearby felt right. Mama C and Ma Marie would love Sophia! Hopefully, the day would come when they could all meet each other.

Seneca's main goal to escape the island hadn't changed, but a secondary plan was forming in her mind. Originally, she intended to leave this place alone. But after meeting these wonderful people, she couldn't leave them here. Two of them she already cared about.

A third was growing on her.

"Can we walk for a bit?" Jax asked.

They slowed to a crawl as they approached the hospital on their way back to the beach house. Both competitors, they had sped by the building the first time. Matched each other stride for stride, until Jax couldn't take it anymore and lost his stride altogether.

Several palm trees were scattered between the beach and the medical facility, which would be perfect for her to use as cover when the time was right. Her biggest worry was that someone would lock the window overnight. It would be best to prop it open now.

"I know we're almost back to the beach house, and this is really embarrassing, but nature is calling and I can't hold it any longer."

Jax had a good laugh over her fictitious confession. "Piss in the ocean! The fish won't tell on you."

"And get soaking wet before dinner? No, thank you."

"You might wanna shower before then. Just sayin'."

"Just turn around while I duck behind one of these palm trees."

As soon as his back was turned, she made a beeline for the hospital. At least she wouldn't waste time actually relieving herself. When she was close to the building, she grabbed a palm tree leaf and tore it into strips.

Jax yelled from the beach. "You don't have to hide behind the farthest tree possible. I won't look."

Seneca ignored him and peered inside the room. It was empty. She examined the lock, then stuffed in a few pieces of greenery. A sufficient job. It wouldn't hinder a person from locking the window, but it would make it easier for her to open later.

"What's taking you so long, girl? Creating some of your own logs for the bonfire tonight?"

Seneca ran up beside him. "That is truly disgusting."

"You're right, actually. I'm not sure why I said that."

They laughed all the way back to the beach house. Jax's sense of humour wasn't always in the toilet. Although, he had quite the pottymouth at times.

"Don't even think about skipping the bonfire tonight. It's going to be fucking epic!"

"Can't wait," she said, walking up the back deck and smelling her armpits. "But right now, it's definitely shower time."

Jax was right.

She needed a good rinse.

"I'm serious," he yelled over his shoulder as he jogged away. "Epic! Promise me you won't miss it."

"I won't miss it. Promise. See you there."

CHAPTER 35

THE ISLAND BONFIRE

Seneca didn't see Jax at the bonfire. Not at the beginning of the party and not at the end. There were several people missing that night. Including Nick, who famously never missed a Monday night beach party.

The hike was more gruelling than she expected.

From the moment they arrived, she understood why the islanders made the trek once a week. Why they pushed through brush and tripped over tree stumps to get there. They did it for the view.

Finally, something truly heavenly.

A waterfall!

Sparkling rapids cascaded down the side of a cliff. Caves tucked in behind. On the beach next to the waterfall, orange and yellow flames rose high into the sky from a raging bonfire. Island residents had built seats around the firepit using wood and stones. Four tiers in a circle. A place to congregate for fun and fellowship.

"This is like a scene from a movie. I would say I'm speechless but I'm not. I have a million words to describe this picturesque setting."

"I've painted it a million times," said Sophia. "Mostly in my mind. Sometimes on canvas."

"Let's check out the caves," suggested David.

The trio explored the caves. Swam in the pool at the bottom of the waterfall. Then they dried themselves off, so they could warm up before the sun went down. The bonfire helped immensely with the warming up part.

The sky was clear.

If a storm was on the way, this was definitely the calm beforehand.

"He's not here, David. You said he would be here."

Carol Morgan sat down next to them.

"It's still early, Carol. Jax isn't even here yet."

"Those two cuties always come together. You know that, babe."

Carol appeared slightly comforted by David and Sophia's words. "I suppose you're right. Nick and Jax always show up a little late. A little tipsy on that moonshine. Have you tried Nick's stuff lately? I'll never admit it to his face, but it's tasting surprisingly good."

The woman's words bled into the background. Seneca couldn't pay attention. She was awestruck by her second true sunset. It was more inspiring than the first. Last night's sky had been bright orange and yellow. Tonight, those colours were joined by bursts of blues and reds.

As darkness settled in, she turned to Sophia. "Is there a special washroom around here?"

"Men usually go off to the right." Sophia pointed away from the beach. "Women to the left. Need a friend?"

"No, thanks."

She met one anyway.

"Oh, I'm so sorry! I didn't see you there."

This was definitely the most embarrassing moment of her life. In the dark, Seneca had leaned against a pee tree that was already in use.

"No worries at all, doll."

"Did I get you?"

"Well, my left sandal is a bit damp. Coulda been me, coulda been you. We'll never know for sure."

"Hi, I'm Seneca."

They skipped shaking hands.

"Kay Johnson. Nice to meet you."

She recognized the name. "You haven't been here long."

"Four months."

Kay's Light Ceremony was back in March. The 26-year-old had also made it to the seventh step. Which meant she had also fallen through the floor of the glass box.

"Your arms healed up nicely," she said, examining Kay's shoulders and triceps. "Hope I don't end up with too many scars."

"I suffered twice as many cuts as you did. You'll be fine."

It turned out they were practically neighbours. Kay had recently moved into one of the smaller log cabins built for one. It was located a few cabins down from the beach house, where she spent her first three months with David and Sophia. Kay spoke highly of her former hosts but treasured her alone time.

On their walk back to the bonfire, they ran into Carol Morgan.

"Kay! I've been looking for you. Have you seen Nick?"

"Which one is Nick again? Sorry, I'm still trying to keep everyone's name straight."

"Dirty blonde. Thirty. Deep dimples. Always trying to start that stupid conga line at the bonfires."

"Yes, of course! I know exactly who you're talking about," said Kay. "Unfortunately, I haven't seen him around. Not for a few days."

"If you do, would you ask him to get in touch with me? I'm worried."

"Sure thing. I'll let him know right away."

Carol took off into the woods.

Kay's eyes narrowed.

"Everything alright?" asked Seneca.

"Yeah, just something Carol said. I hadn't thought about it much, but I haven't seen my neighbours Benoit and Valerie since Friday. They've never taken off anywhere without letting me know. Not even to dinner."

"That's sweet. Kind of."

"I thought the same thing. A little overbearing, but sweet. Now their lights have been out since Friday and I didn't even question it. I'm a terrible neighbour!"

"Don't feel bad. You've been through a lot."

A group of dancers moved in sync next to the fire. Kay scanned the crowd for her friends.

"Ben and Val love to dance. They might be over there. I'm going to see if I can spot them."

"Good luck. It was great to meet you."

"Samesie. See ya."

Seneca walked down to the shoreline. She removed her sandals and stuck her toes in the ocean. To anyone passing by, it might appear as though she didn't have a care in the world.

That couldn't be further from the truth.

How was she supposed to stay focused on planning her escape when islanders were going missing? First Nick. Then Kay's neighbours. Even Jax, who had been so adamant that she not miss the bonfire, hadn't shown up tonight. Something odd was afoot.

Part of her wanted to be selfish. To ignore what was happening on the island and focus on her own situation.

But she couldn't.

Whoever was responsible for the missing islanders held the key to unlocking the door to her freedom. She was sure of it.

All she had to do was figure out who was holding the key.

Find them.

And take it back.

CHAPTER 36

TENSION AT THE BEACH HOUSE

Seneca waited impatiently in her temporary bedroom her hosts to settle in. It had been a long night and it was late.

Why weren't they going to bed?

David and Sophia had been talking in the kitchen for over an hour.

Tonight was the night she planned to scope out the hospital. If she had to wait much longer it would be pouring by the time she managed to sneak away.

Rain wasn't the real problem though.

The real problem was staying awake. She was getting tired and there was no alarm clock in her room. Even if she had one, she wouldn't set it for the middle of the night. It could wake David or Sophia.

If they ever decided to go to sleep.

"I don't care what you say, David. This is not normal!"

They were arguing.

Seneca tilted an ear into the hallway.

"It is normal, Sophia. People have gone missing before."

"Not at this rate! Not people like Nick and Jax."

"We don't even know if Jax is missing. Seneca was just with him this afternoon. Why is everyone jumping to conclusions?"

"Conclusions? Don't be an ignorant fool."

"We need to be calm, Sophia. No good comes around these parts when people get all riled up."

Sophia was having none of it. She told David she was going to march up to the hospital and demand to speak with Dr. Joe tonight. Something about finally getting some answers for herself.

"Don't be so impulsive. Please, just this once. Going to the hospital late at night is the stupidest thing you could do."

"Don't talk down to me, David. I'm not a child."

"Far from one," he said, then muttered. "You got even farther away the last time you got this excited."

"Don't go there. That's low."

"Dammit, Sophia!" Seneca had never heard David raise his voice. "You've been here almost twenty years. By now, you should have learned something about the consequences of asking too many questions."

"Consequences no longer concern me." Sophia's voice was eerily calm. "Time is running out for me, babe."

Heavy footsteps.

Wham!

The front door slammed shut.

Light rain drops struck the windowpane as Seneca watched Sophia storm off.

CHAPTER 37

SOPHIA GOES MISSING

"Why do I even bother? Always trying to be a saviour. Always failing."

Seneca peered into the kitchen. David was muttering to himself. He paced and rubbed his hands together, as though the movement itself would help him reach some critical decision.

"Did I hear Sophia leave?"

"Oh, hey there." David tried to hide his concern. "Yeah, Sophia just went for a walk. I'm sure she'll be back soon."

"What were you saying about being a saviour?"

David dropped the front. He collapsed into a chair and poured himself a glass of alcohol from the bottle on the kitchen table. Seneca wasn't sure what type of alcohol it was. It was brown and he didn't add anything to it. Not even an ice cube.

Head in his hands, fingertips drowning in his brown locks, he resembled a man who had given up. "I don't want to bother you. It's late."

She sat down across the table. "Happy to lend an ear."

For the next twenty minutes, he rambled on about life before his Light Ceremony. David's favourite topic was his wife, Kate. His one true love. The woman he promised a better life.

A broken promise.

David had told her he would move mountains for her. When it came down to it, he couldn't even hold his breath long enough to prove his love. Not to her and not to their unborn child.

"She was pregnant?"

"Only a few weeks along. We hadn't taken a test or been to the doctor, but we both knew."

"I'm so sorry, David."

"That's okay. I remember hoping it was a girl. I would have liked to have had a daughter. Although, I probably would have tried to *save her* from living her life. Some men are always trying to save women. I'm one of them."

"I guess we don't really need saving."

"Nope, most women don't need saving. They're perfectly capable of saving themselves. In fact, some of us men need a good person to save us. As much as we hate to admit it."

"My one mom is certainly great at saving my other mom," she said.

"Yes, of course. You mentioned you were raised by two women. When you yell for mom, do they both answer?"

"I call them Mama and Ma to avoid any confusion."

"That's smart. My sister is a lesbian. She married a woman who is among the best and brightest in the world. A real free spirit, who is more headstrong than anyone I've ever met. Not the type to need saving, that's for sure. The kind of woman who never lets anything or anyone stand in her way."

"I wonder what she's up to now?"

"Good question." David gazed out the window towards the hospital. "Very good question."

CHAPTER 38

HOSPITAL FREAK OUT

"How the hell did you get up here?"

Sophia had strutted past the receptionist, stolen a swipe card off a sleeping security guard and taken the elevator to the top floor. The elevator doors opened into a lavish penthouse. *Surprise, surprise.* The doctor was living the high life.

"Time for the two of us to have a little talk, Dr. Joe."

The doctor stood up from the couch and grabbed a walkie talkie from the coffee table in front of him.

"Kevin. Upstairs, now!"

"Afraid of a little old lady? I just want to talk."

"Leave now, Sophia. Go back home and we'll pretend this didn't happen."

"That's the problem I'm having, Dr. Joe. Every morning when I wake up and look in the mirror, I find it extremely difficult to pretend that none of this happened."

"We've had our fair share of troubles, but Heaven Island is a blessing. You know that. You should be thankful for the second chance at life."

How could he possibly say this place was a blessing?

She lunged at him.

Her fingernails dug into his wrists. They fell back onto the couch. She managed to get in a few good kicks and scratches before he threw her kicks and scratches before he threw her off. She landed hard on the coffee table.

It didn't hurt.

Her adrenaline was pumping.

"Heaven Island is not a blessing. It's a curse!"

"Well, how about we take you over to the dreaded Hell Island. Would you like that? Then you'll regret the day you ever complained about being here."

"Is Hell Island where you're taking all of the missing islanders?"

"Missing islanders?"

"Don't play stupid with me, doctor. It's obvious people are going missing. Not all of them can be swimmers."

The doctor's expression was one of genuine confusion. Maybe he really had no idea why people were missing or where they were going. He did know the terrible thing he had done to her though, and Sophia wasn't about to let it go.

Dr. Joe was ready when she pounced at him a second time. He grabbed her arms and twisted them behind her back. This time, she felt the pain.

"Let go of me!"

He threw her to the floor and pinned her down. "Stop struggling, Sophia."

The elevator doors opened.

"What's the problem, Dr. Joe?" Kevin rushed in and discovered the two of them in a pile on the living room floor.

"Kevin. It seems Sophia no longer wants to live here on Heaven Island. Why don't you take her for a little boat ride and show her what it's like to live in hell."

CHAPTER 39

THE CIRCLE OF LIFE

Sophia's blindfold slid down her face. Kevin untied her feet and lifted her out of the boat. He had cut the engine about a minute before they reached their destination, and by the sounds of it, paddled the rest of the way through choppy waters.

No longer in complete darkness, she scouted out her surroundings.

So this was the dreaded Hell Island?

All she saw were trees and a beach.

The man with no neck placed her into the ocean. He carefully untied her hands. The gentleness of his touch was ironic, considering he was leaving her here to die.

Maybe I can tough it out on my own?

Water pooled around her thighs.

Perhaps there are other survivors!

Waves slapped against the boat. Kevin climbed back in, fired up the engine and gave her a small smile.

Sick bastard.

Then the boat disappeared.

He was gone and she was alone.

Would David come for her? Would Seneca be experimented on? With so many questions racing through her mind, she hadn't noticed all of the glowing eyes shining from along the shoreline.

Then she heard the low growls.

Low growls that expanded into loud howls.

Sophia was brought back to a terrifying reality by a pack of wild dogs. Not just any wild dogs. Ferox Caninovours. So barbaric, they were rumoured to eat their own.

Was this a nightmare?

It wasn't possible. Roxy dogs were supposedly extinct.

But even with her diminishing eyesight, Sophia could see that the deadliest canines to ever walk the earth had not perished.

They had simply relocated.

It was safe to say she wasn't feeling especially welcome in their new home.

The towering beasts were twice the size of regular wolves. They bared their teeth. It wouldn't be long now before they pierced her rapidly aging skin with their fangs. Tore her apart limb from limb.

Soon her body would be scattered across the island. Perhaps one of the Roxy dogs might carry her bones, bits of meat on them, back to the den for her pups to devour?

At least she would be returned to the earth.

The circle of life.

It didn't matter. She only had a few good years left anyway if she was lucky. Dr. Joe had ruined her body with the experiments. A lot of pain came along with aging quickly. Not to mention the emotional toll.

Feelings of hopelessness turned to rage. How cruel life could be!

Fuck the dogs.

Sophia turned her back to the pack and submerged her entire body into the cold ocean. She had no intention of ever resurfacing. There were worse ways to die than drowning.

Like being pulled apart by a pack of Ferox Caninovours.

Underwater, she held her breath and took a moment to reflect. Pieces of her life flashed before her eyes. Most were happy memories. A few painful ones. Some were major life events. Others, as simple as the sunset she had witnessed days before with David and Seneca.

Life had changed dramatically since then.

An image appeared in her mind, going back almost two decades. It was her soulmate. The only person she had ever truly given her heart.

Her wife.

She recalled the moment they met. Caught in a downpour on an early afternoon in late May. Her love's bronze skin, soaked from the rain. Dark hair clung to her strong, seductive physique.

Wise hazel eyes had pierced into her big blues.

Marie was the reason she had decided to become a Light Seeker. To risk it all for a fairytale ending. If only she had known then what she knew now. That she had already hit the jackpot the day they met.

She couldn't hold her breath any longer.

Focused on that first memory of Marie standing in the rain, smiling through a downpour as though she had just stepped outside on a sunny day, Sophia took a mouthful of water into her lungs.

As she did, she was startled by a commotion behind her.

The dogs had come for their dinner.

One of the beasts grabbed hold of her neck with its teeth and jerked her head above the surface. Sophia coughed. The water she inhaled returned to the ocean.

The dogs bit into her clothes. As a pack, they dragged her back to shore.

Apparently they wanted their dinner on dry land.

She expected them to drop her to the ground and dig in, but the Roxy dogs carried her past the tree line. Branches scraped against her body. The beasts tugged her through the dense brush.

Then the trees opened up and Sophia spotted more Roxy dogs. At least fifty of them. All sitting in a perfect circle.

They surrounded one man, who stood with his back to her.

It didn't matter that his face wasn't visible. She would have recognized him anywhere. His hair was longer now, but the dreadlocks were a dead giveaway. Not to mention he stood nearly 8-feet tall.

The dogs carried her into the middle of the circle and released her at the man's feet. Sophia landed with a thud.

That would leave bruises.

Exhausted and in pain, she looked up and whispered his name. "Micah."

•———•

Micah Xander looked down at the woman the Roxy dogs had dropped at his feet. He had trained the dogs not to rip people apart. However, teaching them to be gentle seemed an insurmountable task.

The woman resembled a friend of his from Heaven Island, though she was much older. Had it been that long since they had seen each other? No, his eyes must be deceiving him.

Those big blues though.

Micah hadn't seen Sophia in years, but he knew those eyes.

But how could she have aged this rapidly? This woman had gray hair and her skin was covered in wrinkles.

Then Micah was struck by the devastatingly obvious.

They had experimented on her.

She reached up for his hand. Micah grabbed hold of her wrist and pulled her to her feet, then beyond, with a quick flex of his giant arms.

Forget the dogs. Maybe he was the one who needed a lesson in gentleness.

"You were always so strong," she said with a faint giggle.

That was definitely her voice.

"Sophia?"

"That's me. Now before you say it, I know what you're thinking. It's been a while and it looks like it's been even longer for me."

Micah held his weakened friend to his chest. What had she been through on that dreaded island since they had last seen each other?

They could discuss that later. He needed to get Sophia back to the caves for medical attention and a good sleep.

Yes, rest first.

They could recall the past after some much-needed downtime. More importantly, they could plan for the future.

A future that no longer included Heaven Island.

CHAPTER 40

MILDRED FINDS A NEW HOME

Thursday, April 27th, 1972

Mildred was in shock. Had she really just heard her father's most trusted advisor order two soldiers to 'get rid of her'? Even at age seven, she was wise enough to know Walter Crow had ordered them to kill her.

Rattled, Mildred could only think of one thing to do.

Run.

No harm would come to her sister. Walter needed a Queen. He had said so himself. It pained her to leave her sister, but she knew it was her only chance of survival.

The young princess reached out and pressed her hands against the laundry room wall. She closed her eyes and imagined her twin sitting in their father's chair on the other side. Tears escaped, making their getaway down her cheeks to dampen the vinyl floor.

"I'll come back for you, Tilly," she promised in a whisper.

It was time to go.

The hallway was empty. The two soldiers were off searching for her, and she assumed Walter had returned to the study. The family's secret spot. A room he had zero knowledge of until today.

Still, there was one secret about Jordhar Castle that the head of the Royal Privy Council was not privy to.

The trap door on the closet floor of the King and Queen's bedchamber.

The twins loved to crawl inside, descend the ladder rungs to a spiral staircase that circled down past the basement. There was only one rule. The girls were not allowed to go through the door at the bottom of the stairs.

Mildred had no idea if the door would be locked now, but she knew where it led.

To the tunnels.

The tunnels ran from Jordhar Castle, far north to the forest border. The soldiers had said giants were attacking the military, so she could only assume they had come down from the Northern Forest to protect Barsicon. During bedtime stories, Queen Raya had always portrayed them as caring giants and Mildred desperately wanted to believe her mother's fairytale version.

The stone wall cooled her sweaty palms, as she pressed her body against it for one last barriered good-bye with her sister.

"I love you, Tilly."

Mildred gave the wall a kiss and climbed into the laundry chute. She inched her way up, which was harder than she expected. Sliding down the chute had been much easier and way more fun.

Adrenaline propelled her to the top.

The sound of footsteps and two familiar voices stopped her from throwing open the hatch. It was the men Walter had ordered to kill her. They were in her bedroom.

"Mildred, sweetheart. Are you in here? Your sister is looking for you and she's really worried."

"Yeah, she's so worried. Margaret wants you to…"

Slapping sounds. "It's Matilda, you idiot."

"I don't care what her name is. The princesses are both pompous little bitches anyway."

"They're children, you imbecile."

"Whatever. She's obviously not here. Let's go."

Yes, please leave!

Her arms and legs were starting to ache from holding herself up.

"Wait a second. What if she's hiding in the laundry chute?"

No, no, no! Should she drop back down, or stay still and hope the soldiers didn't open the hatch? Before she had a chance to decide, they made the decision for her.

"If the girl climbed into the laundry chute, she would be down in the laundry room by now. I swear, you're the dumbest piece of shit I've ever met."

As soon as the door closed, Mildred pushed open the hatch and dropped into her bedroom. She yearned to climb into bed. To pull the covers over her head and pretend this was all a bad dream. Just in case, she pinched the skin on her left forearm between her thumb and her index finger.

Ouch!

This was definitely not a dream. It was a real-life nightmare.

She needed to get to her parents' closet.

To the tunnels.

Overwhelmed at the thought of seeing her dead parents again, Mildred started to weep. She grabbed a stuffed unicorn from her sister's bed and held it close to her. It was Matilda's favourite. If she was going to be brave enough to get through this alive, she needed a piece of her sister with her.

Should she leave Tilly a note?

No. Someone else might find it.

Then it dawned on her. Mildred set the unicorn on the floor by Matilda's bed and gathered all of their stuffed animals. She quietly placed the plush toys in the shape of a heart on her sister's bed and laid out a red sweater at the bottom. If Matilda failed to notice the animals were in the shape of a heart, she hoped the bright colour would make it stand out.

The crimson red reminded her of her father's blood seeping into the mattress. Tears started to form again. She held them at bay. There would be plenty of time to cry later.

Mildred snuck into the empty hallway in her slippers and a nightgown, armed with Matilda's rainbow-horned cuddle buddy 'Sparkles'.

If there was anyone in the King and Queen's bedchamber, she would circle back to the laundry chute. That was her plan B.

There was no plan C.

Mildred listened at the door and considered opening it a hair. Then the hair on the back of her neck began to rise.

She was not alone.

Murmurs emanated from inside the room and voices grew louder in the opposite direction. The two soldiers were approaching from the stairway at the end of the hall. In a matter of seconds, they would be able to see her standing out in the open.

"Check her room one more time."

It was now or never. Mildred dropped to her hands and knees. She pushed the door open just enough for her small body to slip through. There were voices coming from the balcony.

"Where did these goddamn giants come from, Walter?!"

General Homer Thomson was arguing with Walter Crow. She wanted to run across the room and kick him. Punch him. Scream at him for murdering her mother and father. But she couldn't. The best she could do was ignore the General and save herself.

Mildred tried not to look at her parents' lifeless bodies as she crawled towards the closet and watched the scene on the balcony unfold.

Walter held his hands up in cautious surrender. "Homer, I know this looks bad."

"You said my men would be in control at the end of this. You promised I would be King by morning. Now look!" He pointed from the balcony to the streets below. "There are enormous mutants wiping out my troops by the dozens!"

"Give me a chance to explain."

"Explain what? How on the same night we plan a hostile takeover of Barsicon, *giants* start massacring my men and only *my* men? They're not attacking the villagers. Only those in uniform. There's no explanation for this!"

"Yes, there is. Please, let me show you something."

Walter motioned for General Thomson to follow him closer to the edge of the balcony.

"Look north, Homer. What do you see?"

"*General* to you. Have some respect."

"My sincerest apologies, *General* Thomson. What do you see when you look north?"

The General turned his back to Walter and watched the monstrous men move in. The sun was setting in the west. The sky, on fire.

Walter placed his free hand on Homer's back and repeated the question. "Tell me what you see?"

"I see goddam giants taking over Barsicon. A city that belongs to me!"

"Yes, exactly. And that is the last thing you will ever see."

Walter pulled a knife out of his waistband and slit the military leader's throat in one quick motion. General Thomson grabbed his neck. Both hands were immediately blood-soaked.

He tried to speak but gargled his words.

Walter shoved Homer over the balcony and watched his body connect with the pavement below.

"It looks like I'm the General now," Walter howled, a sardonic laugh that would haunt Mildred for years to come.

The princess reached the closet and scrambled to get inside before Walter spotted her. She couldn't risk closing the door. He was walking towards her now and might notice the movement. Instead, she hid underneath a pile of her mother's dresses and prayed he would leave quickly.

From under the soft fabrics, through lace that smelled of her Raya's perfume, Mildred watched Walter walk across the room and spit on the King, who lay frozen on the bed with a hole in his skull. He proceeded to step on the fallen Queen's chest, as though her mother were a carpet, not a human.

And then he was gone.

Mildred counted to sixty before she emerged from the pile of dresses.

Her entire body shook as she struggled to put on one of the King's sweaters. She would need it to keep warm. The gray, wool pullover grazed her ankles. She needed one more thing before she could leave. Sparkles was a piece of Matilda. She had her father's sweater. Now she needed an item that belonged to her mother. But what should she take?

The diamond tiara veil!

The one Queen Raya wore on her wedding day.

Mildred scanned the closet for the headdress. It would also serve as a second message to her sister that she had made it out alive.

The twins played dress-up in their parents closet at least once a week. Matilda would insist that when she got married, she would wear her mother's wedding dress. But she would *not* wear 'that hideous tiara'. Mildred loved the tiara veil and jumped at the opportunity to wear it. It made her feel pretty.

"It's all yours!"

She could hear her twin sister in her head.

Mildred placed the tiara on top of her dark locks and caught a glimpse of herself in the full-length mirror. Her swollen aqua eyes were filled with such intense sadness, she almost didn't recognize herself. The diamonds shining through her messy hair added no spark. The veil was twice the length of her body. She wrapped it around her neck and tucked the tulle scarf down the front of her oversized sweater.

Mildred lowered herself into the floor and closed the secret hatch behind her. If a person didn't know there was an opening in the floor, they would never spot it.

The only other person left alive who had knowledge of the secret passageway and the tunnels was Matilda. Hopefully her sister wouldn't tell Walter about the trap door. If her twin spilled the beans, Mildred could expect soldiers on her heels at any moment.

Only one hurdle stood in the way of her fleeing Jordhar Castle. The door at the end of the spiral staircase. The twins had always been told they were never to go through it. Under *any* circumstances. Truth be told, she had always assumed it was locked.

Now she prayed it wasn't.

Mildred stumbled down the final few steps and flew her body into the steel door. It didn't budge.

Come on!

Then it dawned on her. In her haste to escape the castle, she hadn't turned the handle.

The doorknob was cold to the touch. It turned but wouldn't open. Once again, she threw her body against the cold steel. Pain surged through her shoulder and Sparkles fell to the floor, as she bounced back onto the bottom stair.

"Why is this happening?" she cried out.

The castle didn't answer.

For several minutes, she sat at the base of the spiral staircase and sobbed. What was she going to do? She couldn't stay there. She would starve to death. Going back wasn't safe and going forward seemed impossible.

She was stuck.

Then a voice whispered from behind her. "Try the door again."

She turned.

No one was there.

Physically exhausted, she pushed herself to her feet and prepared to try the door one more time. Mildred picked Sparkles up off the floor, turned the knob and pushed.

It still wouldn't budge.

Another faint whisper. "Pull."

Of course! In her panic, she hadn't tried pulling the door open. When she turned the handle and yanked it towards her this time, it moved. The door was stiff from years of unuse. After a few good tugs, she broke through.

A burst of energy surged through her body as she entered the tunnel. She wanted to take off running. To get as far away as possible from the people who had slaughtered her parents and wanted her dead.

However, as soon the door closed behind her, any urges she had to run were suppressed by the darkness.

The dark scared her. Matilda had always been there to make her feel safe.

Now, she was all alone.

For the next thirteen hours, Mildred walked blindly in her pink slippers through the secret passage. She stopped only for brief naps on the dirt ground, wrapped tight in her father's sweater for warmth. Sparkles doubled as a pillow. Otherwise, it was one foot in front of the other, over and over, until her left foot kicked something.

She stumbled forward.

In an attempt to break her fall, she threw her hands out in front of her. Her palms landed on a set of earthy stairs, formed hundreds of years ago with dirt and rock. The stairs led to the surface, where the forest floor camouflaged a wooden cover.

The tiny, timber exit was the only thing that stood between Mildred and the outside world.

Life in Jordhar Castle was all she had ever known. Now she was about to step into the complete unknown.

Exhausted, she contemplated sleep before continuing on.

Extreme thirst pushed her forward.

Mildred squatted on the top stair. She placed her back against the wooden cover so she could use her leg strength to push it open. Despite years of overgrowth, she freed herself easily.

The difficulty was seeing.

Blinded by the sun in the east, she squinted and allowed her eyes to adjust to the light. After a minute, she stood waist deep inside the hole in the ground and took in the sights around her.

Mildred was in the middle of the Northern Forest, surrounded by massive pines and redwoods. Dirt paths ran through trees and open fields. She inhaled the type of fresh air that only arrives after a heavy rain.

The forest was as magical as her mother described. For a moment, she forgot all about her thirst.

The moment came and went quickly.

Covered in dirt from tiara to slipper, Mildred lifted herself from the tunnel and closed the lid behind her. Parched, she considered drinking the tears of joy that spilled down her cheeks when she spotted a pond in the distance.

"I'll be right back, Sparkles. Don't you go anywhere, okay?"

Mildred propped up her sister's unicorn on a nearby tree branch and set off towards the pond. Maybe she would meet some friendly giants or cute Roxy dogs along the way! If only Matilda was here. She would see that their father's stories about the dangers in the Northern Forest were nothing more than made-up tales, told to frighten her.

When she reached the pond, she unravelled the veil from her neck and removed her father's sweater. Her nightgown would dry quickly. She ran into the water, bathing and drinking simultaneously.

Pure bliss!

Captivated by her new environment, Mildred had no clue she was not alone until a deep voice startled her back to reality.

"Excuse me."

A giant stood on the verge of the pond. Not the giants from her bedtime stories. This one was bald and covered in tattoos. He had a ringed beard long enough to graze his groin. In one massive fist, he held a machete. In the other, he clutched Sparkles the unicorn.

"I think this belongs to you."

PART 3

CHAPTER 41

FOREST PROTECTORS

Mildred lowered herself into the water. Her chin grazed the surface. The giant took two enormous steps into the pond.

"I'm so sorry. Please don't hurt me."

"Whose child are you? You speak well for an infant."

"Pardon me, but I am not an infant. I'm 7-years-old and my parents are dead."

"Seven?" he growled. "Then you are not from the Northern Forest."

"No, sir. I'm from Barsicon."

"Young girl, there are rules for your people," he bellowed. "Under no circumstances are you allowed to enter the Northern Forest. The penalty is death. Everyone knows that. Do you have a death wish?"

Mildred hesitated. If she told him she was royalty, he might kill her anyway.

Or could that save her?

With no time to mull it over, she blurted out the truth. "I am Princess Mildred Jordhar of Barsicon. I escaped certain death during a takeover at the castle. Since then, I have come to understand there is no safe place for me."

If only her lower lip would stop quivering.

The warrior took another step forward. His massive frame blocked the sunlight from touching her skin as he towered over her.

Mildred winced. He reached down and picked her up by the back of the neck. When she was five feet off the ground---

"Dad?"

The giant released his grip. Mildred's body hit the water, just as a young boy came into view.

He was a miniature version of his father, minus the beard. The pint-sized warrior was shirtless and wore a black leather kilt. Several weapons were holstered in plain sight across his body. His lack of chin hair gave him a youthful appearance. Still, he was as tall as any man Mildred had met in the city.

"Lucah! What are you doing here? Get back home and help your mother with lunch."

The boy raised his chin, not cowering to his father. "I followed you here to learn about being a warrior. To learn how to protect the forest, like you do. I caught fourteen squirrels this morning and gave them to mom. That is more than enough! Please, can I just train with you?"

"You're too young to be a forest protector."

"I'm 10 years old now. That's the same age you were when you took over your first plot of land."

"It was a mere five acres."

"So give me five acres."

Mildred listened to the back-and-forth between Lucah and his father. They seemed to have forgotten all about her. This could be her chance to escape.

"Do you have any idea what it takes to protect our sacred land?"

"Yes, father. I do," replied Lucah. "I'm top of my class and I've never hesitated to follow through on anything."

"Son, you're not ready. Trust me."

The young princess inched her body through the water. She was careful not to create ripples. In her peripheral vision, she spotted the path to the pond. If she could get back to the tunnels, maybe she could hide underground until she figured out what to do next?

Mildred weighed her options.

If she swam to the back of the pond to put distance between them, they would hear her splashing around. Land was less than ten feet to her right. That was her best bet. If she could slither to the edge of the pond and slip out of the water, perhaps she could stay low enough in the tall grass to sneak away unnoticed.

Sparkles the unicorn would have to be left behind.

Fine.

Life was unfair. She was learning that more with each new breath.

Her mother's beautiful tiara veil, gone. Her father's comforting sweater, gone. By the time she reached the verge, salty tears touched her tongue. She washed them away with pond water.

The young warrior continued his passionate plea. "Father, please. I'm ready!"

"Ready to do whatever it takes to uphold the Xander family name?"

"Whatever it takes. Tell me what to do and I'll do it."

Mildred emerged from the water. Goosebumps formed across her skin. The tall grass was still a few feet away. It took every ounce of her patience to crawl, not sprint, towards it.

"This is not a child's game, Lucah. For centuries, the warriors in the Xander family have protected the Northern Forest."

"And I am ready to be one of them. What can I do to prove that to you?"

As if reaching the same conclusion in unison, father and son turned to face the pond, only to discover Mildred had disappeared.

"The girl. Where did she go?" The warrior surveyed the area. "Lucah, help me find her!"

The pair took off in different directions. Lucah headed straight to the water, while his father headed back to the path in the woods.

Mildred hadn't made it to the path yet. The princess lay perfectly still in the tall grass, once again, weighing her options.

What was the point of pushing on?

She couldn't survive alone in the Northern Forest. Besides, most of her family members were dead.

Most of them.

Thoughts of Matilda saved her from losing all hope. Before long, she was back in full survival mode. Down on all fours. Ready to go.

It wouldn't be safe to move forward until she figured out where the boy and his father were. Mildred spotted Lucah fishing around the pond for her. The older warrior was nowhere to be seen.

For the second time that day, the sun disappeared above her.

Noooo!!!

Mildred glanced back and was instantly hypnotized by the warrior's hateful glare. There was nowhere to run. Nowhere to hide. Not willing to give up just yet, she tried to plead with him.

"Mr. Xander, sir," she started. "If you would just let me be on my way, I promise to leave the forest immediately---"

"Lucah, I've found her!" he shouted. "Tell me girl, how did you make it this far into the forest?"

The tunnels.

She couldn't tell him about the tunnels. If by some unlikely chance she managed to escape her current dilemma, the tunnels might be her only safe haven.

"I escaped Jordhar Castle and ran into the streets of Barsicon after my parents were murdered," she lied. "I was fleeing the city with strangers, when a man in a truck offered us a ride. I fell asleep during the journey and woke up here."

"Was the man in the truck one of us, or one of your kind?"

Mildred wasn't a good liar. She hated to fib. But in her current life-or-death situation, the falsities spilled from her mouth like milk from a highchair.

"He was a Barsiconian. A soldier, I believe. He was dressed like one anyway. But he wasn't fighting. Just driving his truck around helping people."

"What did he look like?"

"Brown hair and a big beard."

"A military man with a big beard?"

Oh no! What a stupid lie. Most military men were forced to be clean shaven at all times. Unless they held a high rank.

"I'm telling you everything I remember. He was wearing a camouflage uniform that had an eagle badge on it."

Now that her fake getaway driver had a beard, Mildred would have to make him a colonel at the very least.

"An eagle badge?"

"Yes, an eagle badge and one more thing. He seemed kind. The soldier had very kind eyes," she said, then paused a beat. "Just like yours."

Worth a try, but it didn't work.

The giant Xander picked her up in his clenched fist. He loosened his grip slightly when his son joined them in the tall grass.

Mildred curled herself into the fetal position in the warrior's hand and sobbed. Her fight was gone. It was time to surrender. She had tried and failed. Matilda would forgive her. After all, her twin was the strong one. Not her.

"Lucah, do you truly believe you are ready to defend your own five acres in the Northern Forest?"

"Yes, father. I am ready."

"Very well, then. Take a look around." The warrior pointed toward the pond with his free left hand, while Mildred whimpered in his right. "The watering hole will be the centre of your land. From this day forward, it will be your responsibility to protect this area. From our home in the west to the blackberry bushes in the east. Your five acres will run south to the Roxy dens and stretch to the fourth row of pines north of where we stand."

"Yes, father. I am ready."

"You will kill, or be killed, to protect our people and our land."

"Yes, father. I am ready."

"So saith thrice, and it is so. Now, let's see if your words ring true."

The warrior dropped her without warning. Mildred's body hit the ground so hard it knocked the wind out of her. Lucah and his father stared down at her, expressionless, as she struggled to catch her breath.

Why was her body fighting to survive when her mind had let go?

A loud horn sounded out in the forest, taking only Mildred by surprise.

"Lunch is ready, son. Make it quick."

"Yes, sir."

"I'm starving and you know how your mother gets when food goes cold. I'll meet you back at the house."

Mildred's fighting spirit returned. She had no chance against his father, but Lucah was a boy. A big boy, yes, but still a boy. Perhaps she could convince him to let her go. Or she could turn it into a game of chase and ask him for a head start. Boys loved playing games! Then she could sneak back to the tunnels---

"One more thing, Lucah."

"Yes, father. Anything you ask."

"Bring me her head. Feed the rest to the dogs."

CHAPTER 42
A HELL ISLAND REUNION

Tuesday, July 12th, 2022

"Should we head for shore or ride it out?"

Marie had to make the call, and soon. It was well past midnight and stormy weather was catching up with them. If the winds grew stronger, it wouldn't be safe for them to sail to the island.

It was now or never.

"Let's get close to shore and see if we can find a place to dock."

"Sounds like a plan. What if we can't find a spot to tie up?"

Marie knew the answer to Catherine's question, but didn't like it. "We'll have to stick with Fee Fee for the night."

They couldn't leave the sailboat and paddle to shore in a dinghy. Fee Fee would be long gone by morning. The anchor wouldn't hold.

A wave of nausea struck when she thought about riding out the storm. The sick feeling disappeared the moment Fee Fee's masthead light shone on their saving grace.

A dock!

Did that mean there were people here?

If so, hopefully they were friendly.

If they weren't, hopefully she had enough guns to scare them away.

"Prepare the dock lines and attach the fenders. We're going in!"

Marie's brother taught her to sail as a young teen and one piece of advice he gave her always stuck.

"Never approach a dock faster than you're willing to hit it."

She brought Fee Fee to a crawl and prayed there was enough room under the keel. Normally, she would check to ensure they wouldn't hit bottom, but there was no time.

Lightning flashed and thunder roared. Drizzle turned into droplets and their rain jackets did little to help.

Somehow the wet found its way in.

Catherine unhooked herself from the jackline and jumped onto the dock. "Throw me the dock lines."

Marie tossed the ropes overboard. There were no cleats on the dock to tie off on, but there were six pilings, three on each side.

"Please use a bowline knot. I want Fee Fee to be here in the morning."

"That was one time!" Catherine exclaimed. "I was in a hurry."

The dinghy was packed with supplies. Mostly weapons, a couple of blankets and a flashlight. The items were bundled together and wrapped tight in a tarp to keep dry.

Now, to get them to a dry spot.

"I spotted a cave just ahead. Let's check it out."

Out of the rain, they wrung out their clothes and changed into dry garb. Marie set a tarp on the ground and placed a blanket on top of it for comfort.

"Come sit."

Catherine plopped down, took a big swig from the thermos and passed it over. "Coffee?"

"Yes, please."

The two women sat huddled in the back of the small cave, using each other's body heat more for comfort than warmth. They would survive. It wasn't that cold. In fact, now that Marie was dry and wrapped in a blanket, she was quite comfortable. She took a mouthful of java and swished it around, enjoying the temperature. The taste.

"We're so close, Catherine."

"Hard to believe after all these years. Do you think Seneca will understand?"

A low growl.

Both women froze in place.

Marie shone a flashlight towards the entrance of the cave. "Hello. Is someone there?"

A brief hush.

Then sticks rustled and they heard the growls again.

"Pass me my gun," she whispered.

Catherine dug inside their bag for what seemed like an eternity. When she finally produced the gun, Marie took the weapon and handed her the flashlight.

"Keep it pointed at the entrance. I need to see what's coming at me."

It was not at all what she expected.

As Catherine directed the beam of light towards the cave entrance, she saw a massive dog crawl into view.

Not a dog, a wolf.

No, not a wolf. A Roxy dog?

I must be hallucinating!

She wasn't.

The growling grew louder and Marie raised her gun. It was the beast or them. The animal inched closer. She took aim. Trigger finger set---

"Stop! Don't shoot!"

A young man with dirty blonde hair and deep dimples stood at the entrance to the cave. He called off the dogs and held his arms up in full surrender. There was something familiar about him.

Of course!

He was a past Light Seeker named Nick. But how did he get here? Marie was trying to wrap her mind around his sudden appearance when another familiar face strutted in.

Jax?

Yes! They were getting close now.

Her shoulders relaxed. "Nick and Jax, right?"

The men nodded. "Do we know you?"

Marie lowered her gun to her side. "No, but we know you. My name is Marie and this is Catherine. We came from The Darkness to find our daughter."

"I might know her." Jax smiled. "Know a few women around these parts. What's her name?"

Catherine frowned. "Her name is Seneca and she's sixteen. I hope you don't know her."

Once again, Jax had misread the situation. "I do know Seneca! Met her Sunday on Heaven Island."

"You know our daughter?"

"Yeah, for sure. We went for a run on the beach less than twenty-four hours ago."

"Stop it," said Catherine. "Are you serious?"

"Wouldn't lie about such a thing ma'am," said Jax. "In fact, a few of my friends are planning to take a little trip back to the island very soon. You're welcome to join us."

"Your friends? Are there more of you here?"

"Oh yeah! A couple hundred more." Jax helped Catherine to her feet. "Something tells me you ladies will recognize more than a few faces."

It was a short walk through the rain to the leader's cave. On the way, Jax and Nick filled them in on what they knew about Hell Island. Both of them had only recently arrived.

"Remember a Light Seeker from eighteen years ago named Micah? He was so big, people said he was half man and half warrior."

Who could forget Micah?

"Yes, I remember his Light Ceremony. He's here?"

"Micah *made* here," said Jax. "We're almost at his place now. It's just around the bend."

The Roxy dogs trailed at their heels. Their looming presence wasn't especially comforting. When they arrived at the cave, the dogs stopped in their tracks and lay down at the front entrance.

"Follow me," said Jax.

Micah's cave didn't resemble a cave at all.

The walls were covered with paintings and tapestries. There were shelves full of books. None of the furniture matched, but there was so much of it! Couches and recliners. Tables and chairs. Carpets of all different shapes and sizes lined the ground.

It was evident Micah had been on the island for many years, but how he had managed to gather so many creature comforts was a mystery.

"Micah, are you in here?"

A deep voice called out. "In the bedroom."

Jax escorted them to the back of the cave, where they spotted a massive man helping an older woman to her feet. He was about to hand her a cup of steaming liquid.

"Here you go, Sophia. Drink this tea. It will help you feel better."

Sophia?

It couldn't be.

Catherine recognized her right away and threw herself into Sophia's arms before the tea could get there. "You're alive! I knew it. We knew it!"

Sophia looked like she was seeing ghosts. "I must be dreaming. Are you two really here?"

"Yes, we're here. It's us!"

"How did you find me? I don't---"

Catherine cut her off. "What about David? Please tell me he's still alive."

Sophia's expression changed from disbelief to relief, as reality started to sink in.

"Yes, Kate. David *is* alive, and he's just as handsome as the day you married him."

Marie was overjoyed by the news. Her dear brother was still alive! What had happened to her wife though? Two decades had passed since they'd seen each other. Yet somehow, Sophia appeared to have lived four decades or more since then.

"Is it really you?" She cupped Sophia's face in her hands and scanned the deep lines on her flesh.

"Yes, my love. It's me."

"I always knew I'd see you again someday."

"You probably didn't imagine it quite like this."

Marie pushed back a few wild gray strands that had fallen in front of Sophia's beautiful blue eyes. "Does it surprise you that it's raining out there?"

"Not at all, babe. Not one little bit."

CHAPTER 43

NO-NECK COMES CALLING

The storm petered out midmorning. Sophia was still missing.

Seneca and David scoured the cafeteria for their friend at breakfast time but came up empty handed. They left without eating.

Something was definitely off.

"Where are you going?" asked David. "I'm about to make us a snack. You haven't eaten since last night."

She couldn't tell him her plan to snoop around the hospital. "Just stepping out for some fresh air. Maybe a quick walk."

"I don't think it's smart to go wandering off alone right now. Maybe it's best if you stay here with me. Or I can go with you? Either way, we really should have a bite first."

She sat at the kitchen table. David whipped up two egg salad sandwiches on rye and cut them at a perfect angle. The man was very particular and she respected that. Past Light Seekers understood the art of perfecting a task. Even if the task was as simple as making sandwiches.

Two bites in, there was a knock at the front door.

David jumped up from the table. "Stay here! I'll answer it. Maybe it's Sophia and she lost her key."

She finished half of her sandwich in one bite and picked up the other half, ready to throw it down the hatch, while David answered the door.

"What do you mean Seneca needs to go with you?"

Kevin?

"Dr. Joe sent me here to bring her to the hospital."

Something about the results of her blood test.

She scarfed down the rest of her lunch and met them at the door. "You need me at the hospital?"

No Neck nodded.

Perfect.

Now she could walk through the main entrance instead of climbing through a window.

"Wh-why don't I come along?" suggested David. "You know, uhhh, keep the girl company."

Kevin shook his brush cut.

His chin touched both deltoids.

Where was this dude's neck?!

"Thanks for the offer," he replied. "But that won't be necessary."

CHAPTER 44

THE AGING CHAMBER

When she arrived at the hospital, Dr. Joe was waiting for her at the front entrance. He led her to an empty examination room on the first floor, handed her a hospital gown and told her to remove all jewelry. When Seneca was done changing, she followed him to the second floor, where she was about to step into another glass box.

The transparent chamber reminded her of the glass box on the seventh step, except this one had an automatic door and was surrounded by computers.

Hanging on the wall beside it, inside a little glass box of its own, was a switch. The box was locked.

It must be an important switch.

Someone had gone to great lengths to ensure it wasn't pulled by accident.

"Go ahead. Climb on in."

No good came the last time she entered a box like this. But according to Dr. Joe, her blood tests showed disease and this would be her saving grace.

"What kind of disease?" she inquired.

"You don't need to worry about that, Seneca. We have the most advanced medical equipment ever made right here on Heaven Island. All you have to do is step into the chamber, I'll flip the switch and heal you. Then you're free to go."

Free to go.

He kept saying that. Yet there was no truth to it. She might be free to leave the hospital, but no one who lived on the island was actually free.

There were no windows in the room, only the door behind her and a mirror to her left.

A two-way mirror, for sure.

Who was watching from the other side?

Seneca removed her necklace with the half-heart charm. The one gifted to her on her sixteenth birthday. She had tucked it under her shirt before her Light Ceremony and it was still around her neck when she woke up the next day on Heaven Island.

What was it Marie said when she asked about the other half? Something about having faith that she would discover it someday.

"Please, step inside. This should only take a minute."

Barefoot, she entered the chamber. Dr. Joe clicked a button on his handheld remote.

The door closed and locked.

How had she let herself become trapped? Kevin was the only other person in the room and Seneca had killed a Northern Warrior.

She should have taken him out when she had the chance. Now she was a sitting duck. But it had all happened so quickly. She had no time to accurately assess the threat.

Seneca rattled the walls of the chamber. "Let me out of here!"

Dr. Joe looked fixedly at his computer.

"LET ME OUT!"

Could he hear her screams?

The doctor pecked away at his keyboard. When the information on the computer monitor seemed to satisfy him, he grabbed a key from his pocket and unlocked the small glass box on the wall.

A smile crept across his face and he flipped the switch.

Then Dr. Joe focused all of his attention on her. He stared at her with...amusement? Wonderment? It was hard to tell what was going on in his head.

He watched her so intently, at first, Seneca didn't notice her body changing. The hem of her hospital gown that had, moments ago, grazed her knees suddenly touched her ankles. She screamed.

Her body...

It shrunk!!!

Tiny toes stuck out from beneath the garment. This couldn't be? Seneca opened the top of her hospital gown with miniature hands and gawked at her body.

Dr. Joe shouted delightfully at the two-way mirror. "It worked! I knew it would. Didn't I tell you it would work?!"

So this is what was happening on Heaven Island. They were doing aging experiments and she was their latest test subject.

Seneca was totally freaked out by her childlike appearance.

Just as she had done on a few occasions when she was a child, she threw a temper tantrum.

CHAPTER 45

BARBARA'S SUCCESS

Who could blame the girl for freaking out? It would be strange to suddenly have your body shrink without warning.

Whatever.

Joseph would change her back to normal in a minute. Then tomorrow, Barbara could complete her master plan. It was all coming together exactly as she imagined.

All these years on this dreaded island, countless hours spent with that boring doctor, finally paying off.

She was so close.

President Crow watched the little Light Seeker smash her fists against the chamber. From the words she mouthed, it appeared as though she was yelling for Joseph to let her out.

Sorry, sweetheart.

Not until we know this thing can be reversed.

Sitting was no longer an option. She was too antsy. Barbara rose from her chair and stood in front of the two-way mirror to get a better look.

This was it.

Two decades of work came down to this moment.

If only the girl would calm down for a second. If she continued to act like a caged animal, they couldn't allow her to leave after her final check-up tomorrow.

Not tomorrow.

Maybe not ever.

Okay, here we go. Joseph flicked the switch on the wall a second time. The girl morphed back to her regular size.

So far, so good.

Gun in hand, Kevin dragged Seneca out of the aging chamber and threw her on top of a gurney. He held her down, but not with his hands.

With the threat of a bullet to the head.

Joseph tightened the straps around her hands and feet. Nurse Mary showed up and poked the girl's arm with a needle. They wheeled Seneca out of the room and into the hallway.

The doctor joined Barbara in the room next door.

"Kevin and Mary are transporting her to the first floor to recuperate. We'll run a few more tests tomorrow, but everything looks perfect. We've really done it this time!"

In an unexpected move, she wrapped her arms around Joseph and pulled him in for a deep kiss. He deserved it. The man loved her. For two decades, he spent every waking hour attempting to please her.

Well, he finally did it!

Barbara hadn't felt this elated since the day she walked down the ocean to play with her brother.

A happy day that took a tragic turn.

Obadiah had already forgiven her for the unfortunate events that happened that day. Soon, her daddy would forgive her too. How could he not after he saw what she accomplished all on her own? He was going to get his daughter back.

Walter's little Barbie was about to make her reappearance.

CHAPTER 46

HOSPITAL BREAKOUT

It was pitch black when she opened her eyes. Even in the dark, it was apparent she was still inside the hospital.

The smell gave it away.

Seneca was restrained to another gurney. This time, not with loose ropes and basic knots. There were chains around her wrists and ankles, and a strap resembling a belt buckle ran across her midriff.

How long was she out for?

She needed to escape.

But how?

The door handle jiggled. Someone entered the room. If it was Dr. Joe, she was going to spit in his face.

It wasn't the doctor.

"Seneca. Are you in here?"

"David!"

He fumbled his way to her in the dark. When he reached her bedside, David turned on a flashlight so he could see what he was doing. First, he untied the leather strap that bound her upper body. Then he used a set of keys to unlock her arms and legs.

"We need to get out of here," he whispered urgently.

"What about Sophia?"

"I'll come back for her. We need to go now!"

Seneca found her clothes on a chair next to the bed. Her necklace was still inside her pants pocket. If this was the same room where she undressed, that meant it was the same examination room they had brought her to yesterday for tests.

"I know how we can get out of here," she said. "Follow me."

She slipped into the room across the hall. The window was wide open.

David appeared behind her and tossed Seneca a sly smile. "How do you think I got in here?"

She returned the grin. "Was it easy to open?"

"Much easier than I expected, actually. It looked like someone jammed grass into the lock."

Later.

Right now, they needed to get somewhere safe and she had no idea where that might be.

Thankfully, David did.

"The bottom drawer is empty. I checked it."

"Just push the helm and open it," said David. "Trust me."

They had sprinted back to the house along the beach. David had a plan, but he was too frantic to stop and explain it to her. He plucked a bottle of alcohol from the kitchen table, grabbed clothes from the top two drawers of her dresser and asked her to open the bottom drawer.

It was still empty.

"Step aside," he ordered.

David pulled the drawer out completely, exposing a hole underneath the house. "Climb down. I'm right behind you."

Seneca crouched down in front of the dresser and slipped her body through the hole. Rung by rung, she descended the ladder. As promised, David was right behind her, his shoes dropping sand in her hair.

"What is this place?"

David lit a match and fired up a nearby lantern. "I built this tunnel several years ago. Micah used to tell us stories about a tunnel from his childhood. I guess that's what inspired me to create this place after he went missing."

The tunnel was an L-shape. Seneca wondered how long they could last down there, until she turned the corner and saw David's set-up.

They could survive for years!

Now it made sense why David's hands were so calloused, even though he hadn't built a new log cabin in years. He must have been busy expanding this place.

The so-called 'shelter' was almost as nice as the beach house above it. There was furniture. Food. Books. The bunker seemed to have everything Seneca needed.

Except for privacy.

"Where do you go to the washroom?"

"I have a spot around the corner where we first came in. Do you need to go now?"

"No, just curious. Good to know for later."

David slumped into a recliner next to an old couch and popped open the bottle of alcohol.

"Please don't judge me." He took a swig straight from the glass container. "It helps to calm my nerves."

"No judgement here."

He offered her the bottle.

"I'm okay, thanks. Booze might help you clear your mind, but I'm a pretty inexperienced drinker. It would probably cloud my judgement."

Should she tell David what happened to her at the hospital? Probably not. It might worry him more and he already looked like he was about to lose it.

Seneca sat on the couch next to David's chair. "Thanks for saving me. We're gonna figure this out together. Starting with Sophia. Did you keep the keys from the hospital?"

When David climbed through the window to find her, he just so happened to stumble across a set of keys on the desk. The exact keys he needed to get into her room and unlock her restraints.

"Yes, I kept the keys." They jangled as he pulled them from his front pocket. "They're right here."

A gold chain was wrapped around them.

She watched him untangle it carefully. "What's that?"

"The one thing I *always* keep with me. I used to wear it around my neck, but these days it's usually in my pocket."

David turned the piece of jewelry around in his hands. He rubbed it with his thumb and then brought it to his lips.

"I put this necklace on right before my Light Ceremony. I gave a similar one to my wife inside the Waiting Room."

At the end of the chain was a half-heart charm.

"I had them made by a jeweler friend of mine. They're one of a kind. Well, *two* of a kind. I gave one to Kate and told her she would always have half of my heart. The other half, I was saving for our first born."

"Mind if I take a closer look?"

David handed over his necklace. Seneca reached into the neckline of her shirt and pulled out the pendant she was wearing.

"This looks a lot like the necklace my mothers gave me for my birthday."

Seneca removed the chain from around her neck. David eyed her closely. She lined the charms up beside one another and slid them together.

A perfect fit.

One complete heart.

But why would David have the other half of her charm necklace?

"You're sixteen," he said.

It was a statement, not a question, but she answered anyway. "Yes..."

"What are your moms' names?"

"Catherine and Marie. Why?"

CHAPTER 47

MICAH IS ROYALTY

Heaven Island was within their sights. Micah was taking Marie and Catherine there to rescue Seneca and David.

Sophia had insisted on coming with them.

"You've been through so much, my love. Are you sure you don't want to stay here?"

"No way, babe. I'm not missing this reunion."

They rode over in a canoe equipped with an outboard motor. Even with the small engine the trip took almost two hours. The last part of their journey was the most arduous because they had to cut the engine and paddle. It was the only way to keep the noise down.

Now, they were almost there.

On the way, Micah shared adventures from his youth to occupy their minds and pass the time. He was quite the storyteller! All three women were hooked. Even Sophia, who had heard his stories of growing up in the Northern Forest many times, hung on every word.

Micah was the product of love between a woman and a warrior.

"My father was ordered to kill my mother. A test to see if he was ready to become a forest protector. Mom was only seven at the time and father was just ten. It was my grandfather, Zal Xander, who ordered him to do it. He demanded her head as proof."

Sophia had heard the story so many times, she continued it for him. "But Micah's father Lucah couldn't do it. As soon as Zal left, he hid her underground in a tunnel. That's where she stayed for the next several months."

Marie couldn't believe what she was about to ask, but she had to know. "Wasn't Zal upset when Lucah didn't produce her head?"

Micah chuckled. "Poor pops. He ended up telling Papa Zal he had failed. That the Roxy dogs tore the girl apart before he had a chance to behead her."

"Ol' Papa Xander wasn't happy about that!" Sophia chimed in.

"My father was supposed to be given his first five acres of land that day. As punishment, Papa Zal held off on him. So my dad snuck food to my mom. Watched out for her when she needed sunlight or a quick dip in the pond nearby. Eventually, he was given the land and he built a treehouse on it."

"Your mother grew up in a treehouse in the Northern Forest?" asked Catherine.

"Yes, and that's where I grew up. Although the treehouse got *much* bigger over time. As did the area my father protected."

"What an incredible story," said Marie. "Your father saved your mother."

"Yes, and according to my father, I once saved my mother as well. When I was just a baby."

"Really?"

"Apparently, my grandfather came looking for dad one day and discovered the treehouse. He climbed inside and found my mother, huddled in the corner with her back to him. She was cradling something in her arms. Papa Zal was furious! He was about to kill my mom and then he heard me cry out."

"Little baby Micah."

"Not so little. My mother almost died during childbirth. I was born one month early and weighed fifteen pounds and ten ounces! Big baby Micah."

"Micah is an interesting name," said Catherine. "I've never heard it before."

"It's a mix of my mother and father's names. Mildred and Lucah."

"Your mother's name is Mildred?"

"Mildred Jordhar of Barsicon."

"Hold on. Isn't she dead?" asked Catherine.

Marie was confused. "If your mother is Mildred Jordhar, how did she escape the castle during the Battle of Barsicon and make it to the Northern Forest?"

"Through the tunnels."

CHAPTER 48

EXTENDED FAMILY

Seneca looked back and forth between the charms in her hand, and David's stunned expression.

Before she was able to wrap her mind around the significance of the situation, they heard a commotion above them. Footsteps. Someone at the hospital must have discovered she was missing.

"It's okay," said David. "We'll be safe down here. Just don't make any noise."

They heard the dresser drawer open and footsteps descend the ladder. David lowered the wick on his kerosene lantern and swore under his breath.

"This is impossible. Only one other person knows about my hideout."

He extinguished his lantern, but another lantern heading their way shone bright. It lit up the faces of the people coming to get them.

The first person to round the bend was Sophia. An enormous man with long dreadlocks walked beside her.

That must be Micah.

He was followed by the last two people in the world she expected to see. The two women she was fighting so desperately to get home to. Somehow they had found her.

"Ma Marie! Mama C!"

Seneca flung herself at her mothers. They all burst into tears, even Marie, who usually did her best to hold them in. Catherine let go of her and rushed to David.

"My God, David. It's really you!"

How did Catherine know David? Seneca thought about the heart charm necklace he had pulled from his pocket. The one that fit together perfectly with hers. The one he gave to his wife the day of his Light Ceremony.

"Kate. I don't believe it!"

Kate?

David held Catherine for so long, she didn't think he was going to let her go. He ran his fingertips across her face. They shared a passionate kiss. Seneca turned red.

Hold on.

Was Catherine *the* Kate that David had been telling her about?

"Hey bro," Marie slapped David on the back and pulled him in for a hug.

Bro?

Seneca stood in the middle of it all, trying to come to grips with what was happening. Were David and Catherine married before her moms met? But David's Light Ceremony was almost seventeen years ago. Marie had called him bro.

Did that mean?

As Seneca fit the pieces together, she saw Sophia reach out and grab Marie's hand. Their fingers interlocked, just like hers had with Alex back in the orange grove. The way two people held hands when they felt strongly for each other.

"You're probably confused as to who I am." The large man extended his arm. "Micah. Nice to meet you."

Seneca shook his hand.

"I know who you are, Micah." She scanned the room with a quizzical gaze. "It's the others who have me confused right now."

CHAPTER 49

FROM HEAVEN TO HELL

The boat ride back to Hell Island was like a dream. Only three days had passed since she last saw her moms.

It felt like three years.

Should she still be saying 'moms'? Aunt Marie sounded strange. No way she could call her that. Then there was David. Her father. Would he expect her to call him dad right away?

Dad.

It sounded just as foreign as Aunt Marie.

David and Catherine sat in the bow seat, as close together as two humans could possibly sit. In the middle of the canoe, Marie held Sophia, while Seneca and Micah lingered in the stern.

"You okay?" asked the large man with the kind gray eyes.

"I will be."

"I'm sure it's a lot to wrap your mind around."

It was.

Although it explained certain inconsistencies, like her physical appearance. Seneca shared David and Marie's bronze skin, and their almond-shaped, hazel eyes. No doubt about it, she was a Brant through and through.

How long would it take to wade through their stories and find the truth?

"Ma Marie, did you actually meet Mama when you were working on the Ellis family home in Light City?"

"Yes, that's how we met," replied Marie. "David ran the construction company at the time and I was his apprentice."

A helper at his worksite and a witness to *his* love story.

The tale was exactly as they had told her. Except it was David waiting on the other side of the main gates when Catherine walked into The Darkness for true love, donning her flashiest red crop top and skirt full of valuables.

It made sense why Mama C was never really happy in The Darkness. She went there to be with her true love and lost him. David had wanted to provide her with everything her heart desired, and in doing so, he gave it all up.

"Seneca, we're so sorry. We were as honest with you as we could be," Catherine chimed in.

Were you, 'Kate'?

What about the angel who predicted her destiny? That couldn't possibly be true. Even though she desperately wanted it to be. The angel was the magic in her story. The part of her life that existed only because she had faith in it. If nothing else, she hoped her heavenly messenger was real.

"The angel," she asked. "Was there any truth to that?"

"Angel *is* real." Marie turned to Catherine. "Maybe you should take this one."

CHAPTER 50

AN ANGEL AMONG US

Saturday, October 22nd, 2005

"I've made you some tea, Kate."

The old woman handed Catherine a hot mug. Long white hair spilled around her fragile frame, as she lowered herself into a chair next to the fire. Her purple robe, cinched at the waist with a piece of white rope, splayed around the arms of the chair. The outfit was the only one Angel owned, as far as Catherine could tell.

It was the only outfit she had ever seen her wear, anyway.

"You've had a rough night, dear. Let's talk about it."

"A rough night?" she cried. "David is dead!"

Tears fell into her tea.

Angel didn't flinch. "Dead, you say?"

"Yes! After you promised me he would live," she sobbed. "You've never been wrong about anything before. Why this?!"

How could she look so calm? David was dead. Gone forever! Why hadn't she seen that coming?

"Hold on, dear. Let me take a look."

Catherine should be used to this by now, but she wasn't. Witnessing Angel tap into another realm was still as frightening as it had been when she was a little girl.

Years before she was born, Catherine's mother began sneaking into The Darkness for glimpses of the future. She was introduced to Angel as a young child and still remembered the first question she asked the day they met.

"How old are you?"

Mrs. Ellis shushed her, but Angel just laughed.

"I stopped counting at 300," she answered with a wink.

Whether it was true or not, she had no idea. But she knew Angel's predictions always came true.

Until tonight.

Angel drew in a deep breath and closed her eyes. When she reopened them, they were completely white. Her hands started shaking first. Within seconds, her entire body convulsed.

A steady voice, not her own, came through her.

"The future remains the same. Your perception must change. David lives."

David lives?

"Your unborn child will lead you back to him and reunite the people. A baby girl, born to help bring the world out of darkness and into the light. *You* must help her conquer the divide."

Angel exhaled an enormous sigh. The violent shaking stopped. Her purple robe settled and her eyes became visible again.

The old woman was exhausted.

"Train the girl to be a Light Seeker," she whispered. "She will be ready by her sixteenth birthday."

Even for a woman who claimed to have lived many centuries, she looked completely drained.

"Find Marie. Ask her for help." Angel tilted her head back. "I must rest now."

CHAPTER 51

THE ROXY DOGS

"Stay in the boat," said Micah. "I'll lift you out in a second."

"Oh, stop it! I'm fine."

Sophia attempted to stand up in the canoe. Almost immediately, a small wave tossed her back into her seat.

"Dear Sophia, stay in the boat," Micah repeated. "This is my island and that is an order."

A kind, commanding leader. It was clear who was in control around here. The power was all Micah's and Seneca could tell he took that as a responsibility, not a right.

There was sudden movement.

At least twenty people came out of the trees and---whoa!

Was that a wolf?

Micah noticed her wide eyes. "Just a few Roxy dogs. They're friendly enough."

Ferox Caninovours?!

"I've heard rumours they still roam the Northern Forest, but most people assume they're extinct."

"Not even close," said Micah. "I might know more dogs than I do people."

Of the dozen islanders who came to welcome them, David and Sophia knew everyone.

Seneca only spotted one familiar face.

"Jax!"

They shared a hug and he introduced his friend. "Seneca, this is Nick."

"Hey, Nick. Nice to meet you."

David slapped Nick on the back. "Carol Morgan has been looking all over for you, man."

"Really? It's only been two days since Micah showed up to save me."

"Well, you know Carol," he said. "She's a worrier."

"So that's how everyone got over to this island," Seneca concluded. "Micah has been saving you."

"That is how *some* of us got here."

Sophia.

The old woman, who wasn't that old at all, was aging by the second.

CHAPTER 52

BARBARA TURNS BACK TIME

Wednesday, July 13th, 2022

The mirror in the walk-in closet showed every crease on her skin.

Not for long.

President Barbara Crow was ready to get rid of her crow's feet and any other wrinkles that had formed over the years.

Inside her closet, she unzipped a garment bag and carefully withdrew the dress she planned to wear to dinner at Crow Castle. For years, she had dreamed of wearing it again. The pretty pink gown topped with lace.

Her white ankle socks covered in frills and her shiny black Mary Janes would complete the look.

Yes, the outfit was superb.

If only she could try it on!

She couldn't. It didn't fit.

Not yet.

The elevator doors opened. "Darling, where are you? We need to talk. Right away!"

"In here."

Today was the day. It was finally here. Not even Joseph's coddling could ruin it for her.

"There you are, my love. Thank goodness!"

"Why are you so excited, Joseph? Take a breath."

"There is no time! I'm dealing with some major complications at the moment."

Barbara raised an eyebrow. "What is it this time?"

"It's the girl. She's missing."

"Who cares. People go missing all the time."

"I'm talking about Seneca. I went back to check on her this morning and the room was empty."

Why did something always go wrong when she put Joseph in charge? The man was useless. Just when she thought he couldn't do anything to ruin her great mood, here he was, bringing her problems instead of solutions.

With more care than she had ever shown Joseph, she placed her dinner outfit back inside its garment bag. "Follow me."

"Where are we going?"

She crossed the penthouse and stepped into the elevator. "To finish what we started."

"Barbara, we can't move ahead until we find out what happened to the girl. What if the experiment did permanent damage?"

"Someone who is damaged wouldn't be able to escape so easily." She spit out his name. "*Joseph*."

They rode the elevator to the second floor.

"You're not following me. If you enter the aging chamber, you might never come out the same. *Please!* Use someone else to prove the technology works."

"No. It has to be me."

"Why can't you take a criminal from The Darkness and age them? That's why you had me invent this in the first place, to deter criminals. So, use them! Show them what it's like to serve a twenty-year sentence in a day."

Barbara ignored him. She pushed open the door to the room with the aging chamber. Normally, she would be next door, studying their latest test subject from the other side of the two-way mirror.

Today, the tests ended.

The technology would start being used regularly.

Starting with her.

Barbara set the garment bag on the table. Her pretty pink dress wouldn't have to stay inside much longer.

Kevin poked his head into the room but left his body in the hallway.

"Dr. Joe." He noticed Barbara and bowed his head. "Madam President."

Joseph snapped at him. "What is it, Kevin? Please tell me you have the girl."

"We've searched the entire island. No sign of her. Plus, a few others are missing."

Whatever.

The missing islanders were the least of her concerns.

"Fire it up," she ordered. "I don't have all day."

Joseph excused Kevin. "We shouldn't do this, Barbara. The girl is gone and she's not the only one. Something is going on around here and we need to put a stop to it."

Barbara stepped inside the aging chamber. "The only thing we need to put a stop to is our time on this goddamn island. After this, we're done here."

"My love, please. Come on out and we'll discuss this---"

"I said we're done here!"

The fool never listened to her. That's why it took him two decades to figure out the science for this machine and he was still unsure about it! But yesterday, it worked. She had witnessed a teenager convert into a child and back again.

"Barbara, listen to me," he begged. "Let's find the girl and the other missing people, and then we can unveil the project. Push the news conference back a week."

Not a chance in hell. Her big reveal was happening, starting tonight at Crow Castle. There was nothing Joseph could do or say to stop it.

"I don't want anyone else to get hurt, Barbara. I don't want you to---"

"I DON'T CARE! The experiment worked. I saw it with my own eyes. We're doing this. *Now!* Then we are leaving this island and never coming back."

"Fine!" The doctor threw his hands in the air. "I'm tired of arguing with you."

"It's about time," she scoffed.

"How do we play this out? Bring the staff and leave the islanders?"

Barbara thought about it for half a beat. "Bring Kevin and Mary. Leave the rest."

Joseph shook his head in disbelief, but she knew the doctor would do whatever she commanded. His love for her ran deep.

Unfortunately for him, that love would never be reciprocated.

There was only one man whose affection she really craved and she had plans to see him tonight.

"Flick the switch," ordered Barbara. "I don't wanna be late for dinner with my daddy."

CHAPTER 53

A NEW REALITY

Seneca was overwhelmed. In addition to discovering the truth about her family, she was still getting over the shock of being inside the aging chamber. It had been unnerving to watch her body reduce to half its size before Dr. Joe made her 'normal' again.

Was she normal now?

Sophia sat upright, fast asleep, on a chair in Micah's cave.

"I think someone needs a nap," said Marie.

Micah jumped up to help. "Need a hand?"

"No, I'm good."

Just as Marie had done with Seneca many times in her childhood, she lifted Sophia into her arms and carried her wife to the bedroom.

Her wife.

Seneca's aunt.

I guess they were both her aunts, although she would always consider Marie to be her mother. That would never change. Ma Marie had raised her.

They were still blood.

Sophia had lied when she claimed to be a 48-year-old Light Seeker. She was only twenty. But after nineteen years acting as a human lab rat for Dr. Joe, the damage was done.

"The last year has been scary," admitted David. "She's been aging rapidly. At first, we thought it was stress. But then a few weeks would pass, and those weeks would add years to Sophia. Now, she's aging daily."

It made sense why Dr. Joe would experiment on Light Seekers. They were perfect test subjects. All of Barsicon believed they were dead.

But how did he have access to their bodies?

Who created the hole beneath the seventh step?

It had to be an inside job.

"Dr. Joe must be conspiring with someone who has access to the Crow Line," she thought aloud.

"He is," answered Marie. "The doctor is in cahoots with the builder's daughter. I'm sure of it."

"But didn't General Walter Crow build the Crow Line?"

"He did indeed."

President Barbara Crow?

It made sense. There was definitely something unusual about that woman.

But why would the president conduct aging experiments for nearly two decades on a remote island in the middle of the West Ocean?

What did she have to gain?

CHAPTER 54

WALTER'S BARBIE

"There's a blindfold on the door handle. Put it on before you come in."

Daddy was at the door.

"I swear, Barbara, this better be good."

Twenty years of planning and her work was finally complete. She was about to reveal her crime and punishment plan to her father, and simultaneously, win back his affection.

It was perfect.

But was she perfect?

Barbara double-checked her reflection in the mirror above the fireplace. Maybe she should hide in the secret room and reveal herself that way? On second thought, the blindfold was fine.

No need to be dramatic.

The pink lace dress looked just as darling as the last time she'd worn it, on her seventh birthday.

The best day of her life.

'Wally and Tilly', as their friends called them, had thrown a huge celebration at Crow Castle in honour of their little Barbie. There were gifts galore! Hugs and kisses flew around the room.

It was an absolute dream.

Her nightmare didn't start until four days later, down by the boathouse.

Walter jiggled the handle. "The door is locked."

She wouldn't make him wait any longer.

"Leave the blindfold on. Don't ruin the surprise." Barbara unlocked the door. "Come in, daddy."

"Daddy?"

Even with the blindfold on, the General looked tired. His hair, once thick and luscious, was grizzled and thinning. Walter's gut hung over his waistband.

Perhaps her father would take advantage of the technology she created?

Another bonus!

She led him to a chair. "Sit down and lean back."

"Can I take this stupid blindfold off yet?"

"Soon, daddy."

"Barbara, why do you keep calling me daddy? You're acting strange and I don't like it."

Walter began to remove his blindfold and she stopped him. "Just give me a minute to explain. You'll love this. I promise."

It was now or never.

She launched into her plan. "The only way to stop crime is with a strong punishment. I learned that from you, da---, father."

"At least you paid attention to something I said."

Soon, he wouldn't take jabs at her anymore. "As I was saying, strong punishments are needed, and I've created the strongest deterrent to date. I have crime prevention in Barsicon on lockdown."

"Get to the point already, Barbara."

Why was he always rushing her?

Walter was never happy with her, no matter what she did. He was constantly ridiculing her. That's why she worked so hard on this project. To prove to him that she was a real leader and not just his yes-person. To show him that her ideas were revolutionary.

Walter would understand in a minute.

It was almost time to remove the blindfold.

"Imagine a criminal is sentenced to twenty years in prison, but instead of serving their sentence, they serve no time at all."

"We let them go without serving time? Sounds brilliant. I may as well put Obadiah in charge."

"Listen to me, father! I'm talking about serious criminals. Murderers and rapists. The really bad ones we can't send off into The Darkness. We wouldn't have to pay to house or feed them."

Now she had his attention. "Explain."

"With help from the brilliant Dr. Joseph Carter, I have created an aging chamber that can add years to a person's life. No one wants to age rapidly or lose years of their life not having lived it. Let's say someone is handed a ten-year sentence. In the chamber they go and we add ten years to their life."

"What if a person is later found innocent?"

This was it!

The moment she dreamed about for two decades.

"Take off your blindfold."

Walter removed the cloth blinder and saw his child standing in front of him.

"Don't you see, daddy. The aging chamber works both ways."

She clasped her hands behind her back, smiled sweetly at her father and waited for his reaction. It was slow to come.

"Barbara? Is that really you?"

"Yes, daddy. It's me."

When she spoke, he cringed.

"No, no, no," Walter shook his head from side to side. "This is not happening."

"It's brilliant! Don't you see? This is the perfect crime prevention strategy. Plus, we can turn Obadiah into a child again so his mind and body match. He can stay a boy forever."

"This is what you've spent the last two decades working on?"

"Amazing, right?"

Walter hesitated.

"Father?"

There was a long silence before he finally spoke. "It's a waste of time if you ask me. You're freaking me out and you'll freak the people out too."

Wait, what?

"Do *not* let your mother see you like this. I'll tell her you're unwell and can't make it to dinner."

"No, father!"

"We'll cancel tomorrow's news conference."

"Please don't! Just think about it. Life can go back to the way it was before the accident at the boathouse."

"It was no accident, Barbara. You were the accident. You were supposed to be watching your brother and you failed him. Failed all of us."

"But I've worked so hard to make things right. To be the kind of president you want me to be."

Walter scoffed. "I wanted a son to take over my kingdom. You are pathetic. Now get back in that aging chamber and grow up."

CHAPTER 55

SEIZING HEAVEN

Seneca counted eighteen passengers on the sailboat. Fee Fee had never carried more than six, on days when the Coyvilles and JD would tag along for the ride.

Had it only been five days since she sailed the Fennell River?

It felt like a lifetime ago.

But it wasn't. Less than a week had gone by since she celebrated her birthday with family and friends.

With Alex.

One single day was all it took. One special person, one special look.

The song Alex wrote for her played in her mind. What she would give to hear Alex sing it to her again. Seneca thought about them all the time, but Light Seeker training had taught her to focus her attention on the task at hand.

It was imperative that she stay sharp until her mission was complete.

"We should reach Heaven Island in about fifteen minutes," Marie shouted from the helm.

Micah was the leader back on Hell Island, but aboard Fee Fee, Captain Marie was in charge.

Seneca was shocked to find out over 200 people lived on Hell Island, which wasn't hell at all. The gentle giant had built a beautiful community, slow and steady.

He wasn't the first Light Seeker to be dropped off on Hell Island. Many bodies piled up before his arrival.

Micah *was* the first to survive.

When residents of Heaven Island asked too many questions, Kevin took them for a one-way boat ride. The same went for those who were severely damaged in the early stages of the experiments.

No one survived until Micah because of the Roxy dogs. They ruled the island and devoured anyone who invaded their territory.

But the towering beasts with razor sharp teeth didn't intimidate Micah.

The Northern Forest was full of Roxy dogs.

Micah's first job as a child was to help his father Lucah with their pack. So when Kevin dumped him in the water near Hell Island, assuming he would die like all the rest, he lived. Micah rounded up the 'pups', as he called them, and built a shelter.

Then he trained the dogs to rescue the other islanders who were being left to die.

New people.

New skills.

The Roxy dogs became their protectors.

The residents of Hell Island also built a canoe, small enough to hide onshore, but big enough to carry people and supplies.

For several years, they made trips back and forth to Heaven Island. Most of those trips were at night, under the cover of darkness. Micah and his crew would bring back all kinds of items, including furniture, books, clothing and people.

Lots of people.

Seneca was captivated by Micah's stories. She listened intently as he explained his initial anger. He had wanted to kill everyone and everything in sight when he first arrived.

Eventually, his mind outsmarted his inner rage.

Micah realized a fiery rampage was no way to complete a successful takeover of Heaven Island.

It had to be a soft takeover.

"So do swimmers really exist?" she asked.

"The rumours are true," replied Micah. "Some folks were so desperate to leave, they swam away into the unknown. Not all of them though."

As it turns out, most of them were *not* swimmers. Micah rescued them right off the island. By his estimates, he still had seventy-four more islanders to free and he wouldn't stop until everyone was saved.

Now that she was involved, Seneca felt exactly the same way.

No person left behind.

They didn't expect security on Heaven Island to be an issue. The island's remoteness made it secure. Guards were scarce, and the ones there didn't stand a chance against their crew. Not with the weapons Marie had brought along.

She had enough explosives to take down the Crow Line.

Back on Hell Island, Seneca had told them what happened to her in the aging chamber. She kept it a secret at first, not wanting to alarm anyone. But after watching Sophia's body deteriorate so quickly and realizing the technology could give her aunt her life back, she filled them in on every little detail.

David was horrified. "They turned you into a child and back again?"

"It all happened so fast."

"How do you feel?" asked Sophia.

"I feel great. Honestly."

And she did.

Her loved ones looked skeptical.

Marie anchored Fee Fee as close to shore as possible and they went over the plan. The hospital would be their first stop. Hopefully, that's where she'd find Dr. Joe and his sidekick, Kevin. No Neck was their biggest physical threat. If they could eliminate him right off the bat, they would be in great shape.

Sophia was not in great shape.

They needed to get her inside the aging chamber.

Pronto.

They still had a set of hospital keys from David's break-in, so access wouldn't be an issue.

David and the others spread out across the island to send word that help had arrived, while Seneca led Micah, Sophia and her moms up the hill.

Securing the hospital was no problem at all.

The receptionist held his hands in the air the moment they walked in the door, and two security guards followed suit when Marie raised her revolver. They rode the elevator to the second floor and opened the door to the room with the aging chamber.

It was empty.

Seneca turned to her moms. "Stay here with Sophia. I'm taking Micah to the penthouse."

Marie tossed her a knife. "I know your body is a deadly weapon and all, but just in case."

"Thanks. Make sure you clear the room next to us." Seneca pointed at the wall. "That's a two-way mirror."

A quick warning, then she was back in the elevator with Micah and headed to the top floor. Dr. Joe was bound to be there. It was dinnertime and he wasn't one to share a meal in the dining hall.

They heard him blathering as soon as the elevator doors opened.

Was someone else with him?

It would be nice if President Crow and Kevin were there. They could deal with all of them at once. She had a knife, and like Marie said, her body was a deadly weapon. Plus, she had Micah, an 8-foot-tall man carrying several weapons.

This should be easy.

It was not easy. Not easy at all.

They found Dr. Joe alone in the penthouse living room. He'd been blathering to himself. The nearly empty bottle of alcohol in his hand, mixed with his dishevelled appearance, made it crystal clear he was heavily intoxicated.

Drunk as a skunk.

It took the doctor a few seconds to notice they were standing there. "Micah? Seneca? No way. I muzz be dreaming."

"This is definitely not a dream," she said.

"Wurz Barbara?!" cried Dr. Joe.

"You tell us," said Micah.

"I dunno. Sheeez gone."

Micah raised his gun.

"Don't shoot! Pleeeez."

Between sobs, he confessed to everything. Told them what happened earlier that day. How Barbara had taken off in the helicopter wearing a child's pink dress, and how he tried to stop her, but she wouldn't listen.

"Don't you unner-stand! I luff er," he exclaimed between hiccups. "She promised we would be together. Me and Barbara, together. That is what she said. Stupid me believed her!"

Dr. Joe stumbled against the couch and dropped the bottle of alcohol from his hand. *Smash!* In dramatic fashion, he threw his body to the ground and lay sobbing in the mess he created.

"Enough already. Let's go."

Seneca grabbed him by the arm and hauled him to his feet. Micah watched, amused. It was clear she didn't need his help with this one.

"St-stop. Lemme go. Where are you takin' me?"

"Back down to the second floor. There's someone you need to fix."

They heard a noise above.

Chuff-chuff-chuff.

President Barbara Crow was back.

"Slight change of plans." Seneca stepped into the elevator and pressed the button for the roof. "Going up."

CHAPTER 56

BARBARA RETURNS

Why was there a sailboat anchored off Heaven Island?

Something was wrong.

Everything was wrong, actually.

As the helicopter lowered onto the roof of the hospital, Barbara stared down at the ridiculous pink dress she was wearing. Tonight was supposed to be the best night of her life and it had turned into the worst.

Her father was right.

The day at the boathouse wasn't an accident.

She was the accident.

On the flight back to Heaven Island she shed enough tears on her childhood Mary Janes to flood them.

Now, rage replaced sadness.

Barbara was angry at herself. Angry for being so foolish. For wasting decades of her life trying to prove to her father that she was worthy. Obviously she wasn't. Not worthy of his time and not worthy of his love.

Walter had made that clear.

She was so hysterical by the time they landed it wasn't until she stepped off the helicopter and onto the roof that she saw them.

Joseph.

Seneca.

Micah?

How was he still alive? It had been more than a decade since Kevin dropped him off on Hell Island. No one could survive the Roxy dogs. Yet somehow, Micah had.

"It's over, President Crow."

The girl was right. It was over. Barbara had nothing left to live for. Her fight was gone. For all she cared, they could take her away right now and execute her in front of all the islanders whose lives she destroyed for her own purpose. Her own gain.

What had she gained?

Nothing.

Nothing but more rejection.

"You're right, Seneca." Barbara climbed onto the ledge of the hospital roof. "It's over."

CHAPTER 57

THE PRESIDENT'S FINAL FALL

"Please don't jump, Barbara. I love you!"

Seneca didn't want the president to jump either, but Dr. Joe was absolutely distraught at the prospect of his love falling to her death. She had been in the aging chamber, just like Barbara, but seeing her so small was unsettling. All her life, President Crow had seemed so towering and menacing.

Now, she was a child.

A sad child.

"Barbara, come down off the ledge. *Pleeeease*," Dr. Joe begged.

Snot ran down her tiny face. "There's no point. My daddy doesn't love me."

"Who cares! Forget about Walter," Dr. Joe pleaded. "Live here with me. We're all set up and you can be whatever age you choose. Personally, I would love for you to be the beautiful woman you were this morning, before you stepped into that chamber."

Her little body heaved. "I don't want to be any age anymore."

"Please come down," said Micah.

"You don't care if I live or die. Look what I did to you! I left you for dead."

"This is not your fault," said Micah. "Walter is to blame."

She wouldn't hear it. "None of this is my daddy's fault. It's all mine."

Barbara's foot slipped and she waved her small arms to maintain balance. *Was there still some fight in her?* From where they were standing ten feet away, it didn't look like she had much left.

Maybe Micah could convince her to step down?

He knew the truth.

"Your father is not a hero, Barbara. He didn't save Barsicon. He destroyed it. Walter Crow is responsible for the deaths of our grandparents, King Quinton and Queen Raya."

"You're wrong! My daddy is perfect."

"Far from it," growled Micah. "Your *daddy* manipulated your mother as a child and ordered the execution her twin sister, Mildred. My mother."

"No, he would never! Stop lying."

Teensy hands covered wee ears.

"It's not your fault, Barbara," continued Micah. "It's your father's and he will pay. But you don't have to. You're a victim. Same as the rest of us. Now please, come down from there."

Barbara stopped crying.

Good. They were making progress.

But wait.

No, stop.

The president's frilly pink dress twirled in the wind as she turned her back to them and calmly stepped off the ledge.

Nooooo!!!

They ran, but they were too late.

Too late to stop her.

Too late to witness the fall, or the landing.

What they did see when they reached the edge of the hospital roof was Barbara's tiny body resting on the pavement at the front entrance below. The automatic doors opened and closed, opened and closed, opened and closed.

The only movement from an otherwise static scene.

CHAPTER 58

BACK TO BARSICON

Whispers moved quickly in The Darkness about past Light Seekers coming back from the dead.

Micah's muscles, and let's face it, weapons, had convinced the helicopter pilot to take several trips in order to ferry everyone from the islands back to Barsicon. It wasn't long before residents of The Darkness were well aware of the true history of Barsicon, and they were ready to put an end to half a century of madness.

Seneca couldn't believe she was home.

At first, she didn't want to go inside. She wanted to run directly to JD's house next door, until she saw them through the kitchen window.

"Alex!" She threw herself into their arms.

"Seneca, is it really you?" Alex touched her face. "I can't believe you're here right now."

They kissed in front of everyone.

David was the only one who seemed embarrassed. "I see you have a significant other."

"Yes," she introduced them. "Alex, meet my dad."

"Your dad?"

David reached out his hand. "Hi, I'm David. Nice to meet you."

"Nice to meet you," said Alex, confused. "Catherine, where's Marie?"

"She's sailing Fee Fee back with Sophia."

"Who's Sophia?"

"Marie's wife," answered Catherine.

David jumped in. "Kate, it's probably a lot to explain."

Now Alex was completely baffled. "Who is Kate?"

Seneca took Alex by the hand. "We'll get you all caught up later. We don't have time now. Just because we are home safe, it doesn't mean Barsicon is safe yet."

Not until Walter Crow was dealt with.

King? General? Former president?

None of his titles mattered. His reign of terror was over. Walter was a well-cloaked tyrant who controlled others. Manipulated them into doing his dirty work, so he could remain the hero. He created chaos and discord for his own amusement.

But not anymore.

Angel had told Seneca's moms that she was born into this world to help bring people out of the darkness and into the light. It seemed that prophecy extended beyond her family.

It meant *everyone*.

She was confident that it was time to fulfill her destiny, and this time, she didn't feel alone.

When she was training to be a Light Seeker, it felt like the weight of the world was on her shoulders. Everyone was depending on her to succeed, and deep down, she wasn't sure if she could.

Back in the log cabin, looking into the eyes of Catherine, David, Micah and Alex, she was convinced she would succeed this time.

With their help, she couldn't lose.

No one had ever told her it was solely her job to bring people out of the darkness and into the light. Of that, she was certain. She had heard the story many times before. Seneca had always been told that she was born *to help* bring people out of the darkness and into the light.

No one fulfills their destiny alone.

CHAPTER 59

A TRIP UP NORTH

Thursday, July 14th, 2022

The helicopter dropped Seneca and Micah off at the edge of the Northern Forest. The pilot turned out to be a nice guy and was happy to help. Apparently, flying Barbara back and forth between Light City and Heaven Island for years hadn't been that exciting for him.

"I'll wait here until you get back," he shouted, as they disappeared into the tree line.

"Are you sure it's okay that I'm with you? One of the first things you learn growing up in Barsicon is *not* to cross the forest border."

"You'll be fine. This is Xander territory. At least it was eighteen years ago."

The forest was magical. Micah's brutish face lit up when he spotted the treehouse he grew up in.

The kitchen light was on.

"My mother is up there."

The house was built across several trees, more like a tree-mansion. Micah sprinted up the stairs that circled the massive trunk. Seneca could barely keep up with him, and by the time they reached the top, she had to stop to catch her breath.

"We sh-should knock," she panted. "What if someone else lives here now?"

"We're in the Northern Forest. Trust me, she already knows I'm here."

Micah flung the door wide open, and just as he expected, his mother was on the other side waiting for him.

Talk about a badass!

Mildred was dressed in black leather from head to toe. Her long raven-coloured hair had one white streak in the front, like a skunk. Aqua eyes sparkled when she looked up at her son.

"My sweet Micah," she said. "I've been waiting for you."

Micah's father was dead. Lucah was killed during a Light Ceremony. Walter Crow had forced him to fight and he was murdered by a young man who thought he was entering the God of Light's good graces.

A Light Seeker who then drowned on the fifth step.

Roger was his name. Seneca didn't know him, but Micah certainly did. He had rescued Roger two years ago from Heaven Island and considered him a close friend.

Such is life.

After extended hugs all around, they sat at the kitchen table to brainstorm. Mildred had been formulating a plan to take out Walter Crow for years, she was just waiting for the right moment.

The right moment had finally arrived.

Before they got down to work, they told Mildred about Barbara's death. It clearly upset her. The president was her niece, after all.

"Tilly is going to be so torn up when she finds out," said Mildred. "I have to be the one to tell her."

"Mother, that means going back to the castle. Are you ready for that so soon?"

"Yes, I'm ready," she declared. "Walter Crow has claimed his last victim."

"How will we get there?" asked Seneca. "We can't just walk through the main gates."

Mother and son shared a knowing smile.

"The tunnels."

CHAPTER 60

TUNNEL TAKEOVER

Friday, July 15th, 2022

"I can't believe you walked this far as a little girl, and after suffering such extreme trauma."

"I can't believe it was fifty years ago."

David had mentioned it was Micah's tunnel stories that inspired him to build the shelter under the beach house. She had no idea the stories were true.

But the tunnels were real and they led to the castle. Seneca knew firsthand because she had spent the day walking through them with Mildred.

What was going through her mind?

The woman was about to reunite with her twin sister after half a century, tell Matilda her daughter Barbara was dead, and take down the man responsible for destroying her family.

No wonder she was quiet most of the way.

She did take the time to tell Seneca about her daring escape the night of the Battle of Barsicon, and how she almost gave up at the bottom of the stairs when she was so close.

Mildred reached the door first. "This time I'll remember to push, not pull."

It opened easily.

They wound their way up the long spiral staircase to the trapdoor. Mere steps from the top, they heard Walter shouting.

"Someone find Barbara. Now!"

Seneca lifted the trapdoor enough to see two of Walter's henchmen rush off. They wouldn't find Barbara.

Not alive.

Walter yelled at someone else in the room. "The Light Ceremony is tomorrow night. She needs to be there!"

Matilda walked into view and sat on the bed.

Seneca held Mildred back. "Don't! It's not the right time. You've waited too long for this."

"Way too long," whispered Mildred. "My patience is running thin."

"The guards will be coming for him soon. Let's stick to the plan, okay?"

"Okay," she responded, reluctantly.

Seneca was struck at how similar Mildred and Matilda looked after fifty years apart. The only difference she could spot was the white streak that ran down the front of Mildred's long black hair. A stress streak, maybe?

There was one other noticeable difference between the two; Mildred had grown into a strong woman, while Matilda appeared sad and frightened.

"She'll turn up, Walter. Barbara always does. When did you last see her?"

"Not since her most recent little stunt," he huffed. "You don't even want to know what she was up to this time, Tilly."

"Perhaps you're too hard on her. She's trying her best."

"We both know her best isn't good enough."

Matilda hunched her shoulders and lowered her head. "I'm sure she'll be back for the Light Ceremony."

"I suppose this is what happens to a woman when she's raised by someone like you."

Matilda apologized. "I've tried."

"Perhaps if you had spent more time with our daughter, instead of doting on your stupid son, she wouldn't be so fucked up."

Not only did Seneca have to hold Mildred back this time, she had to cover her mouth as well.

"Please," she whispered. "Have patience."

Mildred closed her eyes and exhaled slowly into Seneca's hand.

A guard rushed into the room. "Pardon me, General Crow. We have a major problem."

"What now?!" Walter exclaimed.

"It's the people. Hundreds are gathered at the main gates and hundreds more are showing up by the minute."

CHAPTER 61

THE ROYAL REUNIFICATION

Walter slammed the door and stormed down the hallway of Crow Castle. Matilda sat on the edge of her bed and cried. The Queen was so upset, by the time Seneca and Mildred slipped in she didn't bother to look up and see who was standing in her bedchamber.

She was a woman accustomed to having her privacy invaded.

Seneca stood guard at the door and allowed the twins to share an uninterrupted moment together. It was an honour to witness the two queens reunite.

Mildred knelt beside Matilda and handed her a tattered stuffed unicorn. "I believe this belongs to you."

The Queen jumped up from the bed. "Millie!"

"Well, this is Sparkles. But yeah, I'm here as well."

Matilda squeezed her sister tight. "I always knew you'd come back for me."

"I'm sorry it took so long, Tilly."

"It doesn't matter. You're here now."

Emotions filled the room.

Joy.

Relief.

But most of all, love.

The Queens shared a bond time could not sever.

A bond Walter Crow could not sever.

CHAPTER 62

GHOSTS AT THE GATES

Walter stood at the top of the seventh step and looked down at the crowd of people in The Darkness. Thousands had gathered already. More were on their way.

No one appeared ready to storm the gates.

They simply stood there.

Calm as could be.

The sun set in the west, shining light on faces he hadn't seen in years. Faces from beyond the grave.

Jax, with his scar necklace.

Carol Morgan, the only Light Seeker to ever fail on the first step.

Standing front and centre, Roxy dogs on either side of him, was Micah.

Impossible!

Micah was killed in a Light Ceremony eighteen years ago. He had watched him die. Same with Carol and Jax.

Walter was the one who had given the Northern Warrior permission to slice Jax's throat in the first place. Saturday nights were starting to bore him. Why not add a little excitement to the fight?

But Jax hadn't died. Neither had Micah or Carol, and there were more familiar faces as he scanned the crowd.

Nick. Roger. David.

Was that Sophia?

The former Light Seekers stood below with torches in hand.

All very much alive.

"You're supposed to be dead," yelled Walter. "Unless you wish to die a second time, I suggest you leave now."

All souls stayed still.

"I command you to leave at once!" he shouted.

The crowd ignored his order a second time and Walter saw red. "Is tonight the night you wish to die?!"

"We could ask you the same question."

Tilly?

No, that wasn't his wife who just walked up behind him.

This woman's face was framed with a white streak and she walked with a confidence his wife had never owned.

But there was only one person who looked that similar to Matilda and he ordered her killed years ago.

Was it possible?

"Hey there, Walter," she smirked. "You look like you've seen a ghost."

CHAPTER 63

MILDRED'S REVENGE

"Mildred?"

"Surprise. I'm still alive."

As the sun went down over the Crow Line, Seneca took hold of Matilda's hand and led her up the final few steps. She couldn't imagine what her life with Walter had been like. He was a terrible man and she had to lie next to him every night. Gave birth to his children while she was still a child.

Did she have feelings for him?

"Are you okay, Tilly?" she asked.

"I think so," she replied, unconvincingly.

They reached the seventh step.

From the top of the Crow Line, Seneca caught her first glimpse of the crowd below. Thousands of people from The Darkness were there, their faces lit up by the fire of their torches. They were quiet, but their message was loud and clear.

Enough is enough.

The power should be in the hands of the people, not in the hands of one man. Certainly not in the hands of Walter Crow.

"What is this nonsense? Cut it out. As ruler of Barsicon, I command you to return home at once!"

No one moved.

Micah shouted from below. "Your reign is over, Walter."

"You don't decide that," Walter roared. "Now get out of my sight, you mongrel. You're as worthless as your father."

"Tonight, I seek justice for my father's death."

"I guess you're here for Roger then." Walter pointed at the man who stood next to Micah. "He killed your father."

"No, Walter. You are responsible for the death of Lucah Xander, Chief Guide of the Forest Protectors, and you are behind countless other deaths in Barsicon."

A wicked laugh. "Perhaps the next death on my hands will be yours...*again*."

"Not if we have anything to say about it."

Micah looked around at the Northern Warriors.

"Who do you think controls the Northern Warriors?" Walter pounded his fist against his chest. "I do! They are my men. Not yours."

"Not anymore."

Walter turned to his guards. "Arrest him. Arrest all of them!"

Utter stillness.

The guards' inaction pushed Walter over the edge and Seneca braced herself for his impending blow up.

"Look at you pathetic losers. You think you can run this kingdom better than me? Good luck!"

Walter saw his wife standing beside her twin sister.

"And Tilly, look at you," he continued. "Just standing there doing nothing, as usual. You're beyond worthless."

Mildred took a step forward. "That's enough out of you."

"Sorry, Mildred, but you showed up fifty years too late. You ran away and left your sister behind for me to take care of. If anyone is to blame, it's you."

Seneca squeezed Matilda's hand and took a step back. Micah was looking for justice, but from the look in Mildred's aqua eyes, she was seeking revenge.

It might be best to get her twin out of harm's way.

"I am not to blame," said Mildred. "You are! I know you had Homer kill our parents before you took his life."

"Prove it."

"No need. I witnessed it, and I overheard you instruct your men to murder me. What kind of man orders the execution of an innocent girl? A vile man, that's who."

Barsicon was silent.

In the wind, you could hear the crackling of flames from the torches below.

Fire that brought light to a dark night.

"Fine then!" Walter threw his hands in the air. "Go ahead and kill me. I know that's what you want after all of these years, isn't it? Revenge."

Seneca expected a bloody scene to unfold. Mildred was holding back, she could tell. From one fighter to another, she could see the woman was restraining herself.

But why?

This was her chance to get rid of Walter Crow once and for all. To kill him and reclaim her kingdom. Save her sister.

Why was she hesitating?

Mildred eyed her sister, then moved slowly in Walter's direction. He started towards the edge of the wall, but before he was able to jump, Mildred grabbed him by the back of his hair and pulled him to the ground.

Her fist slammed into his jaw. Walter cried out in pain. It was time for him to pay for his sins.

Then something totally unexpected happened.

Mildred let him go.

"A quick death is not revenge when it comes to a disgrace like you." She turned to his guards. "Take him away!"

Two Northern Warriors dragged Walter off the steps, although one could have easily handled the job.

"You won't get away with this!" he screamed.

As the guards hauled Walter off, Mildred gave them one last order. "Throw away the key."

There was a roar of applause from the crowd below. It was the most noise the people had made since they arrived.

After all, they weren't there to create noise.

They had come for peace.

Suddenly, the crowd started to back away. All except one man, who was climbing the steps towards them. Seneca was expecting him.

"All set, Micah?"

"It's time." Micah's grin was wider than Dr. Joe's as he turned to the Queens. "We're going to have to ask you ladies to come down. My crew has a small construction project to complete."

That night, the wall came down.

EPILOGUE

A NEW DAY

Saturday, July 8th, 2023

Scorching heat and not a cloud in the sky.

It was a Saturday.

Another day surrounded by family and friends.

Another weekend without a Light Ceremony.

But this Saturday wasn't just any day. It was a special day because it was Seneca's seventeenth birthday.

They sailed Fee Fee along the Fennell River, knowing at any time they could cross freely into the West Ocean.

It was a new Barsicon.

Undivided.

Walter Crow was locked away for life in the basement of the castle. The Crow Line, and the man who built it, fell on the same night.

Mildred and Matilda Jordhar were in control. Two Queens who vowed to live in their mother Raya's footsteps.

The people were free and the wealth was shared.

Some former Light City residents discovered they preferred a quiet life in The Darkness. It was just called Barsicon now, of course, but there would always be people who referred to certain areas as 'Light City' and 'The Darkness'.

Old habits die hard.

Since JD was no longer training Light Seekers, and computers were no longer taboo for him, he went back to school. Technology was his real passion. That being said, he still showed up looking for 'a fight' every now and then.

Seneca surmised it was his way to stay in shape, and she was happy to oblige, *after* he removed her tracker.

Though he no longer had to protect the woodlands, Micah went back to the treehouse in the Northern Forest.

The people of Barsicon, warrior or otherwise, now protected one another.

Seneca looked around at her loved ones seated aboard Fee Fee. They had been through so much to get to this point and here they were. All of them together again.

Well, *almost* all of them.

David and Catherine were cuddled together in the front of the boat. No surprise. They were rarely seen apart. It was strange at first, seeing her mother with someone else. Super awkward to hear David call Catherine, 'Kate'. But she was getting used to it.

Marie sat next to them, but one person was still missing and she didn't want to get started without them.

There they were!

Just in time.

The companionway hatch slid open and Alex emerged from the galley.

"There you are. We were waiting for you."

That giddy, care-free feeling she felt with Alex from the start was still there one year later. Not to say it was all smooth sailing between them.

Love was a learning experience.

"Is this the one you were talking about?" Alex handed her a bottle of Sophia's favourite champagne.

"Yes, this is perfect."

A toast to Sophia, as they spread her ashes.

Before he was locked away in jail, Dr. Joe did his best to reverse the damage he had done to Sophia. But it was too late. It didn't work. Sophia relished two good months before her health deteriorated and she passed away quietly in their log cabin.

Saying goodbye was difficult.

Marie kissed the urn that had sat on the mantle for the past ten months. Then she tipped it over and sent the last remnants of Sophia off into the breeze.

Catherine raised her glass. "To Fee Fee."

Fee Fee?

"Wait a minute. Fee Fee is named after Sophia?"

Now that the truth was out in the open, Seneca loved to hear stories from the past. Marie told one that day that turned out to be her new favourite love story.

"It was late May. A perfectly sunny day, much like today. I had just left the market with some fresh fruit and it started to pour rain. You know me, I love the rain. So, I stopped to enjoy it and I saw a beautiful woman on the street, desperately trying to cover her paintings from being destroyed by the rain."

"Sophia."

"Yes. When she noticed me standing there, she stopped. A strange look appeared on her face, like, 'How is this woman just standing there enjoying the rain, while I'm freaking out!' I'll never forget it."

Alex squeezed her hand and she gave them a smile. It felt amazing to hear about someone else's love story when she was living her own.

"I can totally see you doing that, Ma," she laughed. "So, what did you do?"

"Ran right over to help her, of course. Then we took cover in the doorway of a nearby shop. We were soaked and laughing at the whole scene. When I finally introduced myself and asked for her name, she said, 'So-*PHI-PHI*-a'. I don't know if it was the cold or nerves, but all I heard was 'Fee Fee', and that's what I called her from that day on."

"A toast to Fee Fee," said Seneca.

They raised their flutes.

A sun shower started.

As their glasses clinked, down came the rain. Rain that hid all of their tears. Tears they would have shed freely anyway.

For it was a new day.

ACKNOWLEDGMENTS

To my editor Brandy Gale, I couldn't have completed this book without you. Thank you for helping me sharpen my writing skills, and for guiding me as this story came to life. I am beyond blessed to have you in my circle, personally and professionally.

Thank you Tim Snyder from Ton-Up Creative, my visual genius. The logo you created, as well as the cover design and map, are out of this world. Exactly where I wanted them to be!

Heaps of gratitude to Shannon and all my first readers (you know who you are!) for tackling the first draft. Thank you all for your unique perspectives. Priceless stuff.

As someone who has never stepped foot on a sailboat, special thanks to Tom and Tracy for helping me bring Fee Fee to life.

The audio version of this story was produced by John Sanfilippo from Tyton Sound. John, thank you for your patience, knowledge, and attention to detail.

To Andréanne (Marie Catherine), thank you for investing in me. Much love, boo.

My dear sister Carol, you're my person and I cherish you more than you will ever know. Thank you for continuously believing in me.

A heartfelt shout-out to my sons, Micah and Seneca, for inspiring me daily. I have no idea where I would be without the two of you. My best guess is in a ditch somewhere. You have my unconditional love, always.

And to you, the reader. Thank you.